VALERIE HOBBS

the LAST BEST DAYS of SUMMER

SCHOLASTIC

ISBN 978-0-545-87559-2

12 11 10 9 8 7 6 5 4   17 18 19 20/0

Printed in the U.S.A.   40

First Scholastic printing, June 2015

Book designed by Jaclyn Sinquett

For Juliet

the

LAST BEST

DAYS

of

SUMMER

1

Lucy sat on the porch steps with her arms hugging her legs and a big black bag over her head.

It wasn't a bag anybody could see. It was the kind you feel when you're in a very deep funk, which is exactly where Lucy was.

She wanted this afternoon, this blazing hot August afternoon, for herself. She wanted to swim. She *needed* to swim.

She needed to spend the day at the pool with Megan, her very-best-in-the-world friend.

She needed not to spend the afternoon making model airplanes with Eddie.

She lifted the edge of the bag and peeked out at the lawn that wasn't. Two weeks ago her father had announced his retirement from lawn care and turned the whole front yard to rocks. Glittery white rocks with dusty green cacti sticking up all over the place like warts on the back of a toad.

"Dogs won't come near this stuff!" he had said, planting the last of the thorny cacti. "Great, huh?"

Lucy had rolled her eyes at her mother, who covered her mouth to keep from cracking up. "Yeah, Dad. *Great!*" A laugh exploded out of her and then her mother was laughing, too, both of them holding their sides and gasping for breath.

"What?" said her father, lifting his hands. *"What?"*

He really didn't get it.

Now Lucy sat staring at the rocks, which glittered back with evil intent.

Her grandmother would not like the new "lawn." She would call it artificial, which is what it was. But Lucy wouldn't have to tell her about it. At Grams's, surrounded by pine trees and cool, clean air, she'd probably forget all about the ugly yard. She couldn't wait to be there.

Meanwhile, there was Eddie.

Lucy twisted her friendship bracelet around and around on her wrist. Megan wouldn't have any trouble making this decision. She would get right up and go into her house and announce what she was going to do.

Megan was brave, Lucy was a wimp. That's the way it had always been and that's the way it always would be.

Like this stupid lawn. Permanent.

Wiping sweat from her forehead, Lucy got up. Sweat beneath her nose and behind her knees, sweat rolling down her back. It was just too darned hot.

"Okay," she said aloud. "Okay. That's *it* then. Wimp no more!"

She clenched her teeth for courage and stomped into the house.

"Mom!"

"Don't yell. I'm right here."

Lucy went into the kitchen, where her mother was sitting at the table paying bills. She looked at Lucy over the top of her red-rimmed reading glasses. "I thought you were gone," she said.

"Well, I'm not. I'm not going." Heart clicking like a cricket in her throat.

"To Eddie's? You're not?" Her mother put her pen down. She took off her glasses and laid them on the table.

Lucy went to the sink and filled a glass with water. "It's too hot!"

"And?"

"*And* I'm going to the pool. With Megan." The water in the glass jiggled in her hand.

Lucy's mother blinked. She blinked three more times before she said, "Does Eddie's mother know this?"

Lucy shrugged. "No."

The kitchen got quiet, as if it were listening for what would happen next. Only the refrigerator droned its usual bored hum.

Lucy's mother sighed, a sigh that came up from a place deep within her and tunneled down her nose. "Lucy—"

"I know. I know. I'll tell Mrs. Munch."

Waldo got up from his spot beneath the table. Thwacking the table leg with his tail, he begged Lucy for a pat.

"What about Eddie?" said her mother.

"What about him?" Waldo needed a bath. Badly.

"He has special needs. You know that. That's why Mrs. Munch hired you this summer."

Waldo let out a long, contented fart.

"Waldo!" they both said. Waldo cocked his head. What was wrong? Turning three times, he settled himself under the table and closed his eyes.

"Are you going to tell Eddie you're not coming over?" her mother said.

Eddie was thirteen. Until this summer he had been in a special school and Lucy had seen him only twice in her life.

But all that had changed.

Lucy's heart thunked. "His mother can tell him."

Her mother sighed again. "I'm sure she can. But Eddie's the one who—"

Lucy looked up at the ceiling, where a spider had built a wispy bridge to the light fixture. She sighed dramatically. "Okay! So I'll tell Eddie."

"It's the least you can—"

"*Okay*, I said." Lucy stomped out the kitchen door and into the carport. What good was being twelve if your mother still ran your life?

She grabbed her bike and pushed it out to the driveway. Pulling her phone out of her pocket, she shot a message to Megan: C U AT POOL.

Swimsuit, towel, sunscreen, water.

She went back inside. Zipping quickly through the

kitchen and up the stairs, she grabbed what she needed and left.

Eddie's house was four blocks from Lucy's, a similar two-story structure with drab gray siding. The one big difference, bigger since her father had redone the front yard, was that the Munches had a green lawn full of wooden toys. There were always at least ten of Mrs. Munch's handmade whirligigs sprouting out of the grass like cartoon flowers.

Lucy leaned her bike against Mrs. Munch's battered blue Volvo and went up onto the porch. She knocked on the screen door, which always rattled no matter how lightly you knocked.

The inner door opened and Mrs. Munch, almost as wide as she was tall, appeared behind the screen.

"Hi, Lucy," she said, smiling. "Eddie's been waiting for you."

She pushed open the screen door but Lucy didn't move.

"I, uh, I can't hang out with Eddie today," Lucy said, her heart hammering. "I have to go somewhere. With my, with my mom."

The lie went immediately to the top of her head and sat there, knitting a headache.

"Oh!" said Mrs. Munch. Her dark eyebrows lifted like wings. "Eddie will be so disappointed. But of course if you have another appointment . . ." Her voice trailed off.

"Yeah, teeth!" Lucy tapped her front teeth, as if Mrs. Munch didn't know she had them.

The sun, laughing maniacally, bore down upon her already-pounding head.

Mrs. Munch's eyebrows landed and she smiled her sad smile. "Don't worry, dear. I'll tell him. Shall we expect you Saturday, then?"

"Oh! No! I mean, I can't. That's the day I leave for my grams's house."

"Oh. Oh, dear."

The waiting sat between them like an itch, until Lucy couldn't stand it anymore. "Well, maybe I can come for a little while. You know, to say goodbye and all."

"Yes," said Mrs. Munch, clasping her hands together. "That would be lovely. I'll tell Eddie."

She reached out and pushed the screen wider. "Would you like to come in for a minute? I've got some cold lemonade."

"No, thank you. I've gotta go." Stepping back, Lucy wiped the sweat from beneath her nose with the back of her wrist. Sweat trickled down her spine, seeped out from under her arms. "Well, goodbye, then. My mom's waiting!" Her voice had climbed like a frantic monkey. Anybody but Mrs. Munch, a sweet lady who was sort of out of it, would hear the lie. "See you Saturday!"

She hopped on her bike and fled.

2

The community pool overflowed with screaming children, splashing water, shouts of "Marco!" "Polo!"

A girl in a bright red Speedo dropped in a perfect one-and-a-half off the high dive.

Lucy scanned the crowd for Megan, finding her right where she expected: beneath the lifeguard chair. Wearing her purple two-piece and round white Marilyn Monroe sunglasses, Megan, shining with sunscreen, was stretched out on her Waikiki beach towel.

Lucy locked her bike to the fence and headed for the changing room. Dodging babies and balls, beach towels and lounge chairs, Lucy didn't hear Megan sneaking up behind her.

Greasy fingers covered her eyes. "Guess who!"

"Marilyn Monroe."

Megan dropped her hands and struck a pose, one skinny hip cocked and a bent arm behind her head. Her hair was the color of plastic lawn flamingos. "All I need are the boobs," she said.

"And that cool dress Marilyn wore," said Lucy. "The floaty white one."

They walked together toward the changing room, Lucy wishing she'd let Megan's mother cut her long, thick brown hair. In this weather all she could do was pull it into a ponytail, which *Seventeen* said was out.

"I thought you couldn't come today," said Megan. "I was SO missing you!"

"You didn't look so sad, gazing up at Hottie Scotty!"

"Scotty the god!" Megan clutched her chest. "Just look at him. He makes me crazy!"

They stood staring at Scotty Bucko, the lifeguard. Scanning the crowd, he swiveled his head toward them.

Megan whirled around. "Ohmygod! Ohmygod! He saw us, like, *drooling*!"

Lucy laughed. "No, he didn't. He's just doing his job. He has to look everywhere." But her own ears and neck felt strangely hot and prickly.

The changing room was cool and smelled of towels left too long in doorless lockers.

"Hurry! Get into your suit," said Megan. "He's on duty for another ten minutes. Then it's that mean girl."

Lucy changed into her despicable navy blue one-piece. No bikinis for her, not until she was thirteen. Her mother made these dumb rules based on nothing. Lucy was boobless. What difference did it make what she wore?

She greased herself up and followed Megan's skinny rear end out to the pool.

They settled themselves beneath the lifeguard chair, Megan stretched out, Lucy sitting beside her.

"So what are you wearing?"

At first Lucy thought Megan meant her swimsuit, which she could see perfectly well. Then she got it. "To the pool party? I don't know yet. What are you wearing?"

"Wouldn't it be cool if I could find a dress like you said?"

"Marilyn Monroe's?" Lucy didn't dare reveal her thoughts. Megan as Marilyn? Was she serious?

"Yeah. I could, like, pad the top or something."

Lucy chewed the inside of her cheek. Could she say what she really thought? She couldn't. "I guess," she said.

The Brennan brats ran up, screeched to a stop, and like a couple of wet dogs shook their hair all over Lucy and Megan.

Megan yelped and jumped up. "Evil! You are so evil!"

The twins took off running.

"No running!" proclaimed Scotty from his throne. Sunlight dazzled off the silver whistle dangling down his tanned chest. Even with zinc on his nose, Scotty Bucko was as handsome as a movie star.

Megan's mouth dropped open. She was outright staring.

Lucy nudged her ankle and Megan came out of her trance. Then she laid herself back down.

Lucy closed her eyes. She tried to shut out the shrieks and laughter and let her whole body relax. She would not have been anywhere else for the world.

Except, of course, at Grams's.

"So how did you get out of your job?"

Lucy's eyes snapped open. Her headache came flying back. "I didn't exactly lie, Megan."

"I didn't say you did! Don't get your panties in a twist."

"They're not! I just said that I wasn't coming today, that's all."

But Megan wouldn't let it go. "What did he say?"

"Eddie? He, um, he didn't care."

Now she was lying again and lying made her blush. She hoped Megan's eyes were closed behind the dark lenses of her huge round sunglasses.

Megan yawned. "Yeah, well. It's not like he's, you know, *normal*."

Lucy stared at the glasses, which reflected her own troubled face. Then she looked away, toward the neighborhood and the Munches'. For a moment, a warrior inside her had stood up, ready to defend Eddie. What Megan said wasn't true. Eddie *was* normal.

Well, sort of normal.

And he was sweet. He really couldn't help that he looked and sounded weird.

But the wimp inside her had let the moment go.

Smoothing out her towel, Lucy lay down beside Megan and closed her eyes.

3

That Friday, the Clarence Peabody Recreation Center had been transformed. Cleaned up, washed down, straightened out, the dry grass trimmed within an inch of its life. Not a gum wrapper or soda can anywhere, and the pool looked clean enough to drink from. Japanese lanterns strung end-to-end cast reflections upon the still surface of the water as if they were floating in two places at once.

Against the night sky, the lifeguard's chair gleamed white and majestic, waiting, it seemed, for the true prince. And everybody knew who *that* was.

Lucy and Megan stood outside the chain-link fence, gazing in. They were early. The party would not officially begin for another twenty minutes.

To Lucy's relief, Megan's new white sundress was way more Megan than Marilyn. Lucy, who hated dresses, wore a skirt of Megan's that had a stretchy waist. It was the color of a ripe avocado. Or a muddy alligator. Over it she wore a white tank top. Both girls had sugar-scrubbed their skin until it was scratched pink and ready for perfect fake tans.

They were as beautiful as they could get. Not exactly beautiful, but not exactly not either. A thrill of expectation sprinkled goose bumps down Lucy's arms.

From inside the lighted rec center came the sound of busy grownups. They passed in silhouette across the sliding screen doors, laughing, carrying food and soft drinks from the kitchen, stopping to chat along the way.

From the creek behind the old green building came the sound of equally busy frogs.

Lucy didn't see her father. She guessed he was in the kitchen overcooking the mystery-meat hot dogs and rubbery hamburger patties. Her mother would come later, bringing her famous mushy potato salad. Just last year elderly Mrs. Finch had complained of food poisoning and Lucy's mother had blamed the mayonnaise, and of course herself. She hadn't slept for a week, worrying. This year the mayo would not be added until the very last second.

Megan slapped at a mosquito that was feasting on her arm. "What if he doesn't come?"

Megan's slap startled Lucy, who had been thinking about potatoes and mayonnaise. "Who?"

"Scotty, silly."

A tiny alarm went off inside Lucy. "He has to come, doesn't he? He's the lifeguard."

Megan poufed up her hair. Her lip gloss was as pink and thick as strawberry Jell-O. "He doesn't *have* to. He's his own man, you know."

"*Boy,*" said Lucy.

"Huh?"

"He's not a man, Megs. He's a boy. He's sixteen."

Megan flipped her hand dismissively. "Man, boy, whatever."

"Anyway, he's too old for us."

Lucy wanted Megan to talk her out of that, but Megan only gave her standard answer: "Whatever."

"Hey! There's the band!" Lucy pointed to a white van that had just pulled into the parking lot and parked. THREE FOR ONE, said the dancing musical letters on the side. Doors opened and out came a trio of shaggy-haired men in black slacks and shiny red vests. They unloaded their instruments and carried them toward the rec center.

"Ugh," said Megan. "They're *old*."

"Really old," said Lucy. "But at least it's a real band and not my dad's all-time greatest hits CD."

Megan grabbed Lucy's wrist. "Come on, let's sneak in."

The gate was locked. Megan rattled it back and forth. Then she gave it a kick. "Ow!" she said, grabbing her foot. "They didn't have to lock it! Nobody was going to sneak in."

Lucy laughed. "You're kidding!"

"No, I'm not."

"You just said, 'Let's sneak in.' You are *so* funny!"

"Oh," said Megan, uncertainly. "Well, that's good, I guess. Funny's better than not funny. Funny people can be popular, you know. Let's add funny to our list."

"Ten Top Tips for How to Be Popular" had been one of their summer research projects. With seventh grade and the prospect of an unfamiliar, larger school looming, they intended to be ready.

Not only ready, but ready to be popular.

"Funny would be number eleven," said Megan. "I think we should have twelve."

"Why?" The list had been Megan's idea and most of the rules were hers.

"I dunno. 'Cause it's an even number. Because we're twelve."

A short square figure walked toward them across the dry lawn. "Here comes Mrs. Castro," said Lucy. "Maybe she'll let us in."

"You girls are early," said Lucy's next-door neighbor, unlocking the gate. "And my, don't you look pretty!" she said, frowning at Megan's poufy pink hair.

Lucy and Megan sat side by side on folding chairs. Three for One was taking their first break and the grownups, flushed from gyrating to "I Heard It Through the Grapevine," one of Lucy's father's favorites, were leaving the floor.

"He's not coming," said Megan dismally, her eyes trained on the door.

"Nobody's coming." Lucy chewed the last of the Pinking of You polish off her thumbnail. "We're the only kids here."

Megan stood and smoothed out her dress. "Let's check the parking lot."

"What for?"

"What do you think? He could be out there!"

Lucy smirked. "And what if he is? What are you going to do? Jump into his arms?"

"I dunno. Dumb idea," said Megan, sitting down. "He could be, like, with somebody."

Lucy took a sip of her flat Dr Pepper. "You were in such a hurry to get here! *Nobody* comes early."

Megan dropped her head. "Boy, are we uncool."

Lucy happened to glance toward the door at just that second. "Don't look," she hissed. "It's him."

With a big proprietary smile and his hands on his hips, Scotty Bucko surveyed the room. Everything appeared to be to his satisfaction and he stepped in.

"Sir," he said, striding up and shaking Lucy's father's hand. "Ma'am." He tipped his head toward Lucy's mother, who frowned. *Ma'am*, her mother always said, was meant for old ladies.

Scotty went on to shake a dozen more hands, flashing his super-white smile.

Megan nudged Lucy. "Who's the guy he's with?"

"His brother, Justin," said Lucy.

"How do you know it's his brother?"

"He was in my class."

"Oh," said Megan. "He's cute, sort of. Definitely not Scotty quality, though."

Like his older brother, Justin was wearing a Hawaiian shirt, board shorts, and flip-flops.

"He's really smart," said Lucy. "I mean, *really*. A brain and a half."

"Well, that's good, I guess." Megan pursed her lips. "How's my gloss?"

"Perfect," said Lucy.

After Christmas break last year, Lucy and Justin and two other kids had done a gold rush project together. At first, Justin didn't talk at all. He just sat listening as they brainstormed ideas. Lucy thought he was snobby, but then she realized he was shy. Later they all found out how much he knew about the gold rush. He practically wrote the report himself while Lucy and Diego and Brittney made mountains out of papier-mâché and gold glitter.

The A they got for their project wasn't for the mountains.

Justin glanced around the room and spotted Lucy. His smile was quick and just as quickly gone. Lucy smiled a quarter inch and wriggled the tips of her fingers.

"Ooooo," said Megan. "Crush!"

Lucy's neck heated up. "Not!" she said. "Gold rush. He was in my gold rush group."

"So?"

The band reassembled. "We're going to do some Beatles for you now," said the bass player. Then he laughed. "Well, *our* version of the Beatles. Get out here and dance your fannies off!"

Mrs. Castro grabbed Scotty's hand and dragged him to the dance floor.

Megan jumped up. "Come on!"

Lucy hung back. "What for?"

Up went Megan's long arms, like signal flags. "We're going to dance!"

"We are not!"

But before she knew it, Lucy found herself in the middle of the crowd, dancing and laughing under a cluster of yellow balloons as Megan twirled and spun. "It's been a hard day's night," croaked the band.

Scotty was doing the cool hardly-move thing while

Mrs. Castro bobbed around him like a cork. Megan edged closer to Scotty. And suddenly Megan was dancing across from the super-cool lifeguard, while Lucy bobbed along with Mrs. Castro.

When "A Hard Day's Night" slid into "Lucy in the Sky with Diamonds," Megan raised her arms again and pointed straight down at Lucy's head. "That's Lucy!" she yelled to the band. "THIS IS LUCY!"

"That's my girl!" said Lucy's father. Heads turned. People laughed. Some of them stopped dancing to see what all the commotion was.

Lucy wanted the concrete floor to part like the Red Sea and drop her down to China. Her face burned, her ears pounded. Dizzy, she watched Mrs. Castro leave the floor and come back towing Justin. "You two dance," she said. "I'm beat!"

Lucy and Justin stood like ice sculptures while the band sang over and over and over, "Lucy in the sky with diamonds, Lucy in the sky with diamonds, Lucy in the sky with diamonds." They were never going to quit. Tears gathered thick in Lucy's throat.

Justin scratched his knee. He looked around nervously. He pulled on his earlobe. "You want to go outside?"

Lucy turned and bolted for the door, a hundred miles away.

Lucy leaned against the building with her face in her hands. "That was awful!" she cried. Frogs croaked, cicadas sang *Lucy in the sky with diamonds, Lucy in the sky with diamonds*, somebody laughed. The smell of chlorine drifting from the pool seeped up through her fingers.

When she finally raised her head, she saw that it wasn't Justin who had laughed. On his face was an expression of puzzled gloom.

"Well, it *was* awful!" she said.

His eyes were a deep inscrutable brown, unlike Scotty's pool-water blue. "I know," he said. "I can tell."

"Stop staring at me."

"Okay," he said, and looked up at the sky. "Stars," he said.

Lucy looked up at an ink-black sky filled with stars. Stars as many as grains of sand, they said. Justin would probably know exactly how many. She wouldn't ask.

"I don't know one constellation from another," Justin said after a while. "Do you?"

"You don't?" Lucy checked his face to see if he was kidding.

"Nope."

"Well, that one," she said, "is Orion. See that line of stars? It's his belt. And the one over there? That's Cassiopeia." She had her grandmother to thank for her knowledge of the night sky.

Justin shrugged. "They're all the same to me. Where's the Milky Way?"

Lucy pointed out the swirl of stars that made a path across the sky.

"I guess I wouldn't make a very good astronomer," said Justin.

"What *do* you want to be? I mean, someday."

"An anthropologist," he said. "Or a zookeeper."

They stood for a moment in silence. Then he said: "Do you want to do something?"

"Like what?"

He shrugged. "I don't know. Swim?"

They both turned and looked at the pool. "Can't," she said. "No suit."

"Oh, yeah. Right."

"We could put our feet in."

They went over to the pool and slipped off their shoes. Then they sat and dangled their feet in the water. Justin's feet were long with long narrow toes.

"You have really big feet," said Lucy.

"Thanks a lot."

"Well, you do. That's not a bad thing."

"Well, so are yours. They're bigger than mine!"

Lucy gave him a good hard shove. He laughed and pushed back with his shoulder. Then they were quiet again. It was hard to know what to say to boys. Lucy hadn't had much practice, and Eddie didn't count.

She couldn't stop thinking about Megan. How could she embarrass her like that? But Lucy knew that Megan hadn't meant to. She'd have loved it if the band had sung a Megan song with a hundred refrains. But there wasn't a Megan song. There was only that dumb Lucy song.

Was Megan still dancing with Scotty?

She swirled her feet in figure eights and said into the pool: "Will your brother get mad that we're out here?"

Justin splashed his face, combing the water through his hair. "Probably. He thinks he owns the place."

"He's a really good lifeguard."

Justin frowned. "How do you know that? Did he save your life or something?"

Lucy's face heated up again. She didn't know. It was just something to say. She lifted her feet out and stood up. "Let's go back inside. I don't want to get you in trouble."

Justin looked up. "You won't. We don't have to go in."

"My dad will come looking if I don't," said Lucy, surprised that he wasn't already outside bellowing her name.

They went back across the prickly dry grass, carrying their shoes.

Justin cleared his throat. He cleared his throat a second time before he said, "You don't come to the pool much."

Lucy almost said, like he had, "How do you know?" But that would have embarrassed them both.

Justin pulled his earlobe. "I'm here just about every day. You should come more often. Because, you know." He shrugged. "It's really hot and all."

Was it a blush that crossed his face or a shadow?

"Yeah," said Lucy. "I know."

Lucy stopped at the side of the sliding door and peeked in. The band was playing a slow number. Her parents were draped all over each other and Megan was sitting alone on the edge of her folding seat, looking desperate.

Scotty was dancing with Sharon, the mean lifeguard, like they were one person with four feet.

"Is it okay if we don't dance?" said Justin. "I'm not very good at it."

"I'm not either," said Lucy.

"I'm thirsty from all that swimming." Justin had a one-sided grin that Megan would call goofy, but it was really sort of cute. "Wanna Coke or something?"

"Yes, please. Dr Pepper." Lucy went over and sat next to Megan while Justin went after their drinks.

"Where *were* you?" cried Megan. "I can't believe you left me all alone on the dance floor!"

"Left you?" Lucy's scalp prickled. "What about me? What about making me feel like a total idiot creep?"

"I did not! All I said was—".

"I *know* what you said. And, besides, you weren't alone. You were with Hottie Scotty!"

"Yeah, right," said Megan glumly. "For about one minute."

Lucy looked out onto the dance floor. "Where is he?"

"Beats me," said Megan. "Probably making out somewhere. Like you and your crush."

How could Megan be so mean? Lucy's eyes filled with tears. She blinked them back.

Then Megan's eyes filled. "I'm sorry, Lucy. No, really, I am. I'm sorry for embarrassing you, too. It's just that you're so sensitive sometimes."

"I know," said Lucy miserably.

"You can't be sensitive and popular, you know."

From across the room came an all-too-familiar cry: "LUCY! LUCY!"

Lucy leaped to her feet as Eddie came stumble-running across the room with his chubby arms out. Lucy whirled around, straight into two ice-filled plastic cups of Dr Pepper and Justin, who had been carrying them until they hit the floor, ice skittering in every direction.

"Crap!" he said, dripping Dr Pepper from shirttail to flip-flops.

"Oh, no!" cried Lucy, meaning the mess, meaning Eddie.

Eddie flapped his arms. "Lucy! Guess what? Guess what I got for you? It's in my pocket! It's a go-away present!"

Mrs. Munch stood behind Eddie, carrying a dripping chocolate cake and wearing a lopsided smile. "He never stops talking about you. Lucy this, Lucy that."

Without saying another word, Justin turned and strode away.

Lucy watched him go, her face flaming.

"Come on, Lucy," said Megan, grabbing Lucy's hand. "This party's over!"

Lucy knocked. Mrs. Munch appeared immediately, as if she'd been waiting behind the door. "Hi, Lucy. Thanks for coming. It means so much to Eddie, you know."

"It's just for half an hour," Lucy said, sounding like she'd practiced, which she had. "We're leaving in half an hour for my grams's house."

"Of course, dear," Mrs. Munch said. "Eddie just wants to give you his little present." She smiled down at Lucy as if they shared a special secret. "Ed honey! Lucy's here!"

Lucy went down the hall and opened the door to Eddie's room. It was warm and stuffy. Fourteen model airplanes hung from the ceiling like insects floating through sunlight. Lucy had "helped" Eddie make every one of them.

"Hi, Eddie."

He was sitting on the floor, surrounded by Matchbox cars and orange plastic ramps and roads that didn't connect.

"Lucy!" he cried, stumbling to his feet. He could dress himself now and his green-checkered shirt was buttoned crooked. "Guess what! Guess what!"

"You want to give me something."

Eddie's round face went slack. Then his wide-set eyes lit up. He had beautiful eyes, the exact color of amber.

"Packpack!" he cried. "Mine!"

He went over to his bed, where the straps of a bright red backpack were wrapped around his once-white polar bear, gone gray from slobber.

"Look!" He dangled the backpack in the air.

"Your favorite color," said Lucy. "It's really nice."

"Red! It's red!" he cried.

He laid the backpack on the bed and carefully unzipped it. Then he dumped out the contents. Five-subject spiral notebook, a pack of Bic pens, a plastic ruler ("School Rules!"), and a calculator.

Would Eddie use any of it? He had trouble staying inside the lines of his *Go, Diego, Go!* coloring book.

Eddie plunked himself back down on the floor. He looked up at Lucy, his mouth slack. "Wanna play cars?"

And then that goofy grin. It was hard to say no to Eddie. All summer long she'd been saying yes. Yes to endless games of cars, to Old Maid (he loved the Old Maid card the best). Yes to hide-and-seek, Hungry Hippos, Candyland, games for five-year-olds. But Eddie was a teenager. In three weeks he would be going to Jefferson Middle, just as she would. For at least a part of the day he'd be mainstreamed. He might even be in some of her classes.

Lucy didn't want to think about what would happen

then. Eddie had been her summer job, that's all. And now the summer was nearly over.

"Play cars," he said.

Lucy could not play cars one more time. "Let's paint," she said.

Eddie clapped his hands. "Okay!"

Lucy got out the art supplies and cleared some space on the floor. She laid out a sheet of paper and began to draw.

Eddie craned his neck over the sketch. "What's that?"

"It's a lake," Lucy said. "It's where I'm going to be staying with my grams."

"What's that?" He pointed to the cabin she'd sketched above the lake.

"My grams's house."

Eddie grabbed a blue crayon and drew a box. He added a lopsided roof and the sun above with lines radiating out of it. "My house," he said.

Lucy began to color in her lake, the hearts on her bracelet dragging through the blue paint. She slipped off the bracelet and finished the lake. Then she put her sketch aside.

"Let's write your address," she said. "You can give your picture to your mom for her birthday or something."

All summer they'd been working on Eddie's letters, keeping them more or less in a line.

"Start with a two," she said. They worked their way through Eddie's address, his tongue pushed out in concentration.

"Now you," he said, pointing to Lucy's sketch.

Lucy wrote Grams's address in neat letters along the bottom of her sketch.

"Put the pictures on the wall," said Eddie.

"Please," said Lucy.

"Pretty please with sugar on it," said Eddie, grinning.

So Lucy found the tape and put the drawings on the wall beside all the other drawings they'd done that summer.

"I have to go now, Eddie."

Lucy sat down beside Eddie again so that he would look at her. She needed him to understand that this was her last day. "I'm going on vacation."

Eddie pulled at the back of his upper arm with his stubby fingers and peered down at it. "I had a vaxation," he said. "On my arm."

"*Vacation*, Eddie. It's different. It means . . . well, it means I won't be seeing you for a while. It means I won't be coming over anymore."

He looked up, his eyes golden in the sunlight, but she could see he didn't understand.

"I'm going to my grandma's house," she said.

"Grandma's coming *here*," he said.

Eddie's grandmother, the one who had visited, had passed away in April. Mrs. Munch had warned Lucy not to talk about that grandmother. She would explain things to Eddie, she said, when he was older.

"So I'll see you later, okay?"

Eddie's chin dropped. He began pushing a monster truck back and forth, making an engine sound deep in his throat. His mother had cut his hair again, had hacked it so badly that the hair was all uneven in the back, like Edward Scissorhands had practiced on it. Eddie couldn't see it. It wouldn't matter to him if he could. But it mattered for some reason to Lucy. It made her feel sad for him.

"Later," Lucy said, prompting Eddie to play along. It was how she got away from him, the only thing that worked.

"Alligator," he muttered.

"In a while—"

"Crocodile," he said mournfully, pushing his truck up the ramp.

Lucy stood to leave. At the door she turned, hoping he'd look up, but he didn't. Tears prickled her eyelids and she blinked them away.

Closing his door, she walked quickly down the hall.

"Lucy! Wait!"

When she turned back, Eddie was offering a tiny gray mouse figurine on his palm. "For go-away," he said.

"Thanks, Eddie. It's really nice." Lucy tucked it into her pocket.

"Welcome," he said, rocking his head left and right.

Lucy hurried out the door.

"Wait! Lucy!" cried Mrs. Munch.

Lucy had sailed off the porch on a breath of relief.

She turned.

Mrs. Munch was holding out two crinkled dollar bills.

"Oh, no!" said Lucy, guilt slithering in on its thousand legs. "I only came to say goodbye."

"That's all right, dear," said Mrs. Munch. "Here, take it. You've been so good to Eddie all summer. You've been our lifesaver."

Lucy took the bills. "Tell Eddie that— Tell Eddie—"

"You'll see him in the fall. At school," said Mrs. Munch brightly.

It wasn't at all what Lucy was going to say. What *would* she have said? She didn't really know. But it was *not* about seeing Eddie at school.

Pedaling home, Lucy tried to lose the image of Eddie pushing his monster truck across the floor. She thought instead about all the wonderful things she would do with her grandmother. But it wasn't until she saw Megan that her heart began to lift.

Megan stood on Lucy's front porch, clutching a stack of magazines against her chest. Lucy knew exactly which magazines they were. She had thumbed through them with Megan a hundred times over the summer.

Lucy rolled her bike into the garage. When she came out, Megan pushed the magazines toward Lucy as if she had won a prize. "You'll need these," she said.

Lucy almost said what she was thinking: she would not need the magazines. She wouldn't have a second to look at them. She'd be way too busy doing things with Grams. But Megan's face showed how hard it was for her to relinquish her precious collection.

Lucy took the magazines. "Thanks, Megs. These are great."

"Well, you're going to be bored to death. Things are

different now that you're twelve." As if they weren't the same age, almost to the day. "You'll see."

A lump rose in Lucy's throat as she looked for the millionth time at her best friend. Except for the hours with Eddie and the one short family vacation to Catalina Island, she had spent the biggest part of every day that summer with Megan. If not at Lucy's or at the pool, they were at Curlup & Dye, Megan's mother's salon.

Lucy reached for Megan and they hugged with the magazines between them.

"Wait!" Megan said, breaking free. "I've got something else."

She took back the June issue of *Seventeen* and opened it.

"Ta-da!" she said, holding up a brightly decorated sheet of paper. TWELVE TOP TIPS FOR HOW TO BE POPULAR was written in multicolored letters across the top. "Look at number twelve." She ran her finger under the sentence as she read it aloud: "Don't be caught dead with dummies."

It was Lucy's second chance to defend Eddie, but she didn't take it. "You're such a good artist, Megan," she said instead.

"No, I'm not."

"You are! I wish I could do something artistic like this. Something beautiful."

Megan rolled her eyes. "Okay. *So*. We're both going to memorize these rules, okay? Then they'll all come naturally from the first day."

"Lucy!" Her father had the engine running and the window rolled down. "Let's get this show on the road!" Her mother closed the hatchback and got into the passenger seat.

"Well, have fun!" said Megan doubtfully.

Lucy began backing away. "See you in seven days!"

"I'll quiz you tonight on the phone!" cried Megan after Lucy had climbed into the back seat and opened the window.

She stuck out her head. "What quiz?"

"The rules! Twelve top tips!"

"Oh!" said Lucy. She looked down at the rules. Megan's beautiful designs were smeared with the sweat from her hand. With her other hand, she waved until Megan was a pale pink-topped spot in the distance.

7

Eddie sat on the front steps of his gray house watching the whirligigs. Lucy had come to play with him that morning and now she was gone.

She had gone to a lake, the one she drew a picture of especially for him. The lake had very blue water. Not like the water at the pool, which had a different color he couldn't remember the name of right now.

He clutched the bracelet more tightly in his sweaty hand. Lucy would be so sad that she didn't have it. Probably she would cry.

He wanted to go to that lake and be with Lucy. He would take her bracelet back to her. She would be so happy. And then she would probably take him for a boat ride. He had never ever been on a boat, not once. His mother said, "Maybe someday," which is what she always said. But maybe someday never came.

He got up and went to the garage, where his mother was painting a bird that she'd made out of wood. The bird was lake blue with a dot of yellow for an eye. When his mother finished the bird, it would sit on top of a red stick and whirl around in the front yard.

"Hungry?" she said. "Ready for your snack?"

"Nope," said Eddie.

"Would you like to paint?"

"Nope," said Eddie.

His mother rinsed her paintbrush in a water glass and wiped her hands on the *Star Wars* T-shirt that used to be his favorite. "Are you sad, sweetheart? Are you sad because Lucy's gone?"

Eddie shook his head. He bit his bottom lip to help keep his tears inside.

He looked down at his brand-new blue-and-white running shoes. The left one was good but the right one had a big black smear across the toe.

Now the tears were coming out of his nose. "I hate these stupid shoes," he said, and kicked the tire of the old blue Volvo. "I hate this stupid car."

"How about a snack?" said his mother in her baby voice, smoothing the hair out of his eyes. "Some nice graham crackers and milk."

Eddie kicked the tire again. "I hate snacks!" he said, and went back to the steps to wait for Lucy. If he watched the street and four cars went by, and he counted to one hundred without one mistake, Lucy would come riding back on her bicycle. She would say, "Guess what? I didn't go to the lake." And then she would take him to the station where the dog buses drove in and out. They would sit on the bench and she would stay as long as he wanted.

And he would buy two Popsicles with the money from his piggy bank that had coins and paper money in it.

A red car without a top went by. "One," he said, holding up a finger to help him remember.

He remembered lots of important things. Like his address, 242 Fortuna Street, Goleta, California. His mother had taught him how to say it, but it was Lucy who had taught him how to write it. The whole thing. He wrote the whole thing on the picture he'd made of his house.

A blue truck went by. "Two!" Up went two fingers.

Could a truck count as a car, or was that cheating? He worried about that for a while. Then a white car drove by and then almost right away another white car and he was holding up four fingers.

He went down the walk, all the way to the curb and looked up the street as far as he could see.

No Lucy.

Then he remembered what else he had to do to make her come back. "One," he began. "Two, three, four, five . . ."

8

"Oh, no!" cried Lucy.

"What?" said both her parents at once. Her father glanced into the rearview mirror. Her mother turned her head around.

"My bracelet!" Lucy held up her wrist. "I left it at Eddie's!"

"Oh," said her mother, turning back. "You can get it when you get home."

Lucy groaned. "It'll get lost. Eddie's room's a mess. I'll never find it."

"Of course you will," her mother said.

"Can't we get it now?" Lucy pleaded.

Her father yelped. "Are you kidding? Turn around and drive six hours for a silly bracelet?"

"It's not a silly bracelet," said Lucy, flames of anger heating her cheeks. "It's important. Megan gave it to me."

"Call Mrs. Munch," said her mother. "Ask her to save it for you."

But Lucy didn't want to give her mother the satisfaction of coming up with a good suggestion. She sat with her arms crossed, pouting.

She was tired of riding in the back. Why was she the only one who had to? She couldn't read or even text without feeling carsick. For hours she'd had to look at the backs of her parents' heads, her father's Dodgers cap and her mother's perky hair, which was turning gray. Just a little, but it made her look older than Megan's mother, whose hair was usually blond.

She asked to stop for a cold drink.

"We're almost there," said her father.

"Does that mean no?"

"It doesn't mean yes."

"More condos!" said her mother as they left the highway. "I can't believe it. Pretty soon that's all there will be. Cookie-cutter houses."

Her father was driving slowly, looking for the turnoff to his mother-in-law's house, which now seemed to have disappeared into the new development.

"You passed it," said Lucy, spotting the small cluster of pines that hid the Crescent Lake Drive sign. Her father made a U-turn and went back.

"Ah, this is better," said her father as they crested the hill. "No more building."

"Yet," said her mother gloomily.

They drove the rest of the way in silence, Lucy clearing the window made cloudy by her breath and rubbing her naked wrist.

"There it is!" she said, but her father had seen the little house first—Grams called it her cabin—and was turning into the unpaved driveway. They bumped their way to the top.

"Grams!" Lucy leaped out of the car the second it stopped.

Her grandmother stood in the doorway, wearing one of her clay-spattered smocks. She stepped out with her arms wide and Lucy flew into them. Grams smelled of clay, as Lucy knew she would, but also of all the other remembered things: lavender, bleach, and something without a name that probably came with being old.

"I wasn't going to throw any pots this morning," Grams said. "But it helped pass the time." She held Lucy at arm's length so that she could get a good look at her. They hadn't seen each other since Christmas. "You've grown, of course."

Lucy made a face. "Only a half inch. I don't think I'm going to get any taller."

"Nonsense. You have to grow into those feet." They both looked down at Lucy's sandals. Lucy's big feet were her one hope that she'd ever get over four-foot-ten.

Then her mother hugged Grams, knocking Grams's glasses sideways. "Susie Q," her grandmother crooned. "It's been too long!" They patted backs like they were burping babies.

Then Lucy's father said, "Luz," and hugged Grams, too. Sometimes he called his mother-in-law "Loosely," but only at home. She'd been a hippie before hippies were invented and some of her ideas were kind of off the wall. According to Lucy's parents, anyway. Lucy didn't think so. Her grandmother was interesting. An artist. A freethinker. All the things that Lucy hoped to be.

Well, *and* popular.

They went into the little house—all one room, with huge open beams and a high ceiling. Above the beams were dark stains from where the rain had leaked through. At Christmas her father had climbed onto the roof, brushed the snow away, and nailed down new shingles. The house was a "shack," he said, "falling down around Loosely's ears," but Lucy loved it. The walls smelled like pine trees. There were rugs scattered all over the rough planks of the floor, and piled on the sagging sofa were afghans that Lucy wrapped herself in when the heat of the day was gone. The same sheet music lay open on the ancient upright piano.

And there was Rudolph. When she was younger, she would pretend to talk to the deer whose head was stuffed and hung over the fireplace. Her grandfather, who had passed away when Lucy was nine, had shot the seven-point buck. Lucy herself had eaten some of the venison.

Now she believed that killing animals for any reason was wrong and planned on becoming a vegetarian. But not this week. Her grandmother's meat loaf was just too good. How a person who did yoga every morning to welcome the sun could be a carnivore was something Lucy didn't try to understand. As far as she was concerned, it was just an example of her grandmother's freethinking ways.

So caught up in the smell and the feel of being back,

Lucy hardly heard the one-sided argument going on behind her.

I'm not happy about . . .

What if . . . ?

Anything could happen, you know . . .

All the way out here! Why on earth you won't move to town . . .

Lucy turned. Her mother was leaning against the sink with her arms crossed. Her nose, long and thin like Grams's, looked pinched and pale. "If she's only sixteen, how much help can she be? How responsible is this person?"

Who was "she"? "This person"? Lucy zeroed in.

Grams silently went between the refrigerator and the long plank table, laying out a late lunch. She smiled at Lucy as if to say, *Don't pay attention to any of this. Soon it will be just us.* She pulled out the chair next to her own, where Lucy's favorite plate had been set.

They each made their own sandwich, saying only what needed to be said:

Please pass the mayonnaise.

Thank you.

Is this ham or turkey ham?

(Sniff) *Are you sure this is still good?*

The argument might get picked up again later on, but for now it was over. Lucy knew the gist of it because it was partly about her. About her safety. Grams's safety, too. But mostly about hers. Except for the overnights at Megan's just down the street, Lucy's only times away from home had been her summer stays with Grams.

After lunch Lucy's father suggested a walk down to the lake. Her mother got up and took her plate to the sink. "All right," she said. "Coming, Lucy?"

"I'll stay here and help Grams clean up," said Lucy, sounding, she thought, very grownup. She didn't want to walk down to the lake with her parents. Her father would say all the same old things about it. *This is perfect! Nature at its finest. Look at the blah blah blah!* And then her mother would say her same old things. *Algae bloom, mosquitoes, blah blah blah. What's that rank smell?*

But it was Lucy's sacred place, hers and Grams's. When she saw it again up close—not from the window, where she could see it shimmering now, but up close—she wanted to be with Grams.

"Suit yourself," said her father. "We won't be gone long."

"Take your time," said Grams. She looked down at Lucy and winked. "Take your time."

"Mom almost wouldn't let me come," said Lucy when her parents were good and gone. "Dad had to talk her into it. He almost didn't."

Her grandmother squirted soap into the dishpan. She put her thin, spotted wrists under the tap and sighed. "I know."

"Sometimes she makes me want to scream!"

Her grandmother cocked an eyebrow. "Do you?"

"What? Scream?" Lucy studied her grandmother's face. She was *serious*. "No!" The idea of shrieking out loud while her mother looked on was both thrilling and horrifying.

"It would help," said Grams.

"What difference would it make?" Lucy sighed. "She'd just keep on being who she is."

Grams chuckled. "It's what we humans do best," she said. "Even when it doesn't work anymore."

Grams washed and rinsed the plates, passing them

over to Lucy to dry. She had made them on her kick wheel. All the plates were blue and tan, but each one had a different design. Lucy's favorite plate had bats flying across it, or so she'd decided when she was four or five. Now, no matter how she turned the plate, the bats were nothing more than streaks of colored glaze.

Lucy told Grams about her friendship bracelet and how her father had refused to go back for it.

"Oh, dear."

"It was just a couple of extra hours."

Her grandmother's eyebrow lifted.

Lucy said, "Well, six. But I might never get it back now!"

"Might you call Eddie's mother?"

"Great idea!" said Lucy, as if she were hearing it for the first time. "Thanks, Grams."

She picked up Grams's old-fashioned phone and called Eddie's house.

Eddie's mother answered on the third ring. "Yes?"

"Mrs. Munch? It's Lucy."

"Lucy! Just a second, I'll call Eddie—"

"No! I mean, please don't call Eddie. I left something in Eddie's room, a special bracelet with gold hearts on it. I'm afraid it might get lost. Would you mind finding it and keeping it safe for me?"

"Of course not, dear. I'll look for it right away."

"Thank you, Mrs. Munch. Thank you *so* much!"

"Now you can relax," said Grams when Lucy hung up the phone. But Lucy wasn't sure she could. How would *she* feel if Megan lost some special thing that Lucy had given her? Like her green gemstone earrings that looked so much like real emeralds?

"We've so much to do this week," said Grams. "There's a new litter of fox kittens on Hat Island. I've never seen fox kittens, have you?"

Lucy's worry drifted away. "Never! Let's take the canoe out tomorrow morning!"

"Absolutely."

Lucy stacked the last plate in the cupboard. "Grams?"

"Lucy?"

"Who was Mom asking you about before?"

"Erika? She's the daughter of the man who brings the wood. You remember him. Oscar."

"Oscar?"

"Yes, the wood man. You remember."

But Lucy had never met the wood man. "No, I don't."

Her grandmother's face clouded over. "You don't? Well, no matter. You'll meet him when he brings the wood." She folded the blue-checkered dish towel over the edge of the sink and stood there, looking out at the lake.

"What about Erika?" Lucy said.

"Oh. Erika. Well, she brings the groceries. Does some cleaning up. That sort of thing . . ."

There was more, Lucy could tell.

"She'll be looking in now and then, like she always does. Only a little more often."

"Because I'm here?"

Grams sighed. "Your mother insisted. It was that or—nothing."

"Oh." With her thumbnail, Lucy scraped away at something that had stuck itself to the sink.

"Don't worry, honey. Erika rarely says a word."

Lucy scowled. What good was being twelve if you were still going to be treated like a child? "My mother doesn't think we can take care of ourselves, does she?"

"She's being extra cautious," said her grandmother. "It's all right. We'll survive it."

10

Lucy's parents were back too soon. When they came in, her father went over to the piano and lifted the lid. "Favor us with a tune, Luz," he said. He winked at Lucy's mother. He thought the way Grams played the piano was the funniest thing.

Her mother frowned a warning at him.

Grams sat down on the piano bench with her hands folded in her lap and her back very straight. She raised her hands up over the keyboard, where they fluttered like hummingbirds. Then she plunked them down hard and began to play "The Old Rugged Cross."

Her father grinned at her mother as if to say, *See?* Then he began to sing. He liked to sing, which was really why he'd asked Grams to play. He didn't care what the song was. As Grams played, he leaned over her shoulder to read the music.

But Lucy knew all the words by heart. She and Grams had always sung together, and Lucy was learning to harmonize. But when her mother put her arm around Lucy's shoulders, she got thrown off-key. Her mother couldn't carry a tune in a bucket, her father said, and he was right.

When it came time for her parents to leave, Lucy walked them out to the car, where her father gave her his prized Dodgers cap to wear for the week. Lucy put it on, pulling her ponytail through the gap in the back.

Her mother grabbed her in a fierce hug, laying her cheek on top of Lucy's head. "Be good, pumpkin," she said. "And be careful."

"Don't worry," Lucy said. But of course her mother would. She would call every night, and her calls would break the spell that Lucy and Grams had woven together. "I'll let you know if anything goes wrong. You don't have to call every night."

To Lucy's surprise, her mother agreed. "All right," she said. She straightened the beak of the Dodgers cap. "You love it here, don't you?"

Lucy nodded.

"This might be the last time, you know."

Lucy stepped away from her mother. "You don't know that!"

When her mother sighed, she sounded just like Grams. If sighs were hereditary, Lucy would someday sound just like that, if she didn't already.

"No," her mother said. "No, I don't know that for sure. But I do know that she's getting old, honey. She can't stay alone in this house much longer."

Go away! Lucy wanted to cry. *Go home! Leave us alone.*

So it was another surprise that when they were gone, she started to miss them. But only a little and only for as long as it took her to turn around. There was Grams's cabin with its dark green trim and riverstone chimney nestled under the pine trees, and Grams waiting at the door.

The very best part of the summer was only just beginning.

11

They slept as they always had in two narrow beds across from each other on the screened-in porch. But for a long time that first night, Lucy stayed awake, not tired enough from the day. She thought about Megan and wondered what she was doing. She saw again the shocked look on Justin's face, his drenched shirt and arms, the Dr Pepper dripping.

She tried not to think about Eddie, which only made her think about him.

She worried about her bracelet.

Eyes open, she lay listening to a pair of owls calling to each other from a tree in front of the house to one in the back. The full moon flooded the porch with silvery white light.

Grams read for a while. Then she took off her glasses, folded them, and set them on the nightstand next to her book. She was reading *Moby-Dick* because she never had. "A dreadful hole in my education," she said. Lucy wondered what could be so important about a big white whale, but she didn't ask. If she did, her grandmother would go on and on about it, and Lucy still wouldn't know.

In the morning Grams's bed was empty and neatly made. Lucy smelled pancakes, the very best way to wake up. She did a pretty good job of making her bed, which she rarely did at home, and went into the kitchen.

Grams smiled. "Good morning, my darling," she said, and went back to turning the golden brown cakes.

Watching her grandmother, Lucy decided this was as good a time as any. "Grams?"

Grams looked up.

"I'd like to be called Luz now. Is that all right?"

The idea had come to Lucy after Three for One and the horrible party. She knew her grandmother had never minded sharing her name. Still, it felt a little like stealing.

"Is it all right? Of course it's all right. It's your given name, after all."

Grams slid three cakes onto the bat plate and set it before Lucy.

Lucy dug into the butter. "Luz is more grownup than Lucy. More *serious*."

"Most definitely. And it means 'light,' you know. I've always liked that."

"So call me Luz from now on, okay?" said Lucy.

"Yes, Luz." Grams brought her plate with a single pancake to the table and sat down. "Is it a permanent thing, do you think?"

One of the best things about Grams was that she understood when something was important to you. She let you talk about it as long as you needed to.

Lucy thought forward to school, to Megan, to the first day and how she would introduce herself to girls she didn't yet know.

Boys, too. Maybe.

"I don't know," she said uncertainly.

"Well," said Grams. "It's something to think about, isn't it? Who we are and what we choose to call ourselves."

Grams got up to pack a lunch.

Deep in thought, Lucy lugged in some wood and set it by the fireplace. "Choose," she said to herself. "I get to choose. Me. Lucy Crandall. Me."

They hiked down through the tall pines to the lake, flat and blue in the early morning sunlight. Lucy carried one paddle and the life vests. Grams carried the other paddle. Her old cloth knapsack with the lunch inside hung from her shoulders.

Except for a man and boy who were fishing some distance away, they had the lake to themselves.

The metal canoe gave a hollow-sounding *thump* as they turned it over. They put their life vests on and tied them.

Lucy climbed in first while Grams steadied the canoe, then got in.

They pushed off. It was a shaky start, but soon they coordinated their paddling and plowed through the water at a pretty good clip.

Lucy spotted the small island only because she kept

turning to look for it. "Aren't we going out to Hat Island?" she said.

"Yes. Isn't that what we said?"

Lucy pointed. "But it's that way."

Her grandmother seemed to be coming back from somewhere else. "Yes. Of course," she said.

They shifted their paddles to the opposite side and headed toward the island.

After a while, Lucy's arms began to tire. It was always farther to the island than it looked. But at last they arrived, giving the paddles a final big shove.

"We're quite a team, aren't we?" said Grams as they shot up onto the rocky shore. "You're a good paddler, Lucy."

"Luz."

"Luz," said Grams. "I might forget again, so I'll apologize ahead of time. I've gotten a bit forgetful. Just little things. Nothing serious."

"I forget to do my homework sometimes," said Lucy, mostly to make her grandmother feel better. It wasn't true. She never forgot. She just put it off sometimes because she didn't feel like doing it.

Grams's hair was pulled back in a long gray ponytail. Lucy liked it best when she wore it in a topknot pierced with chopsticks, but the ponytail was probably easier.

Lucy wondered why her mother had worried so much. Grams wasn't old.

Lucy said in her mind to her mother: *Just look at the way Grams walks with her back straight, her stride long, and her ponytail swinging. She's not old, not one bit.*

Hat Island rose to a peak straight up from the shore. When they had climbed to the top, stopping several times to rest, they could see from one end of Crescent Lake to the other. In the middle distance two smaller islands floated like gray whales.

They sat on a flat rock and shared the water Grams had brought. "Oscar said he saw the kits near their den on the far side," Grams said. "Right down there somewhere, I'd guess. We won't want to disturb them. Should have brought binoculars."

"Did you forget?"

For a second, Grams looked annoyed. Then she saw that Lucy was teasing.

"We'll go down there in a bit," she said. "But we'll keep our distance."

A lizard raced up to Lucy's leg, stopped, and darted away. She and Megan had made great plans for a lizard circus the summer they turned six, but the lizards had minds of their own and then Megan got some guinea pigs, which they taught to float on their backs in a kiddie pool.

"Grams?"

"Luz?"

"Were you popular?"

"Popular? In school, you mean? Oh, I don't think so. I was what you'd call a geek, I suppose."

"You were?"

"Oh, yes. President of the Art and Culture Club. We visited art museums and talked about painters as if we knew them."

"Weird," said Lucy.

"I suppose. Why? Are you popular?"

"I don't think so. But maybe I will be next year."

"Is it a big concern, do you think? Being popular."

"Oh, yes. Really big. According to Megan's sister, it's the *only* thing."

"The only thing," said Grams. "My!"

"Well, not the *only* thing . . ."

Grams frowned. "I guess I don't know what *popular* means these days."

"Sure you do," said Lucy.

Grams shrugged. "*You* do. But, really, I don't."

"Well, it means lots of things." Lucy's mind scrambled for what she thought she knew. How could she and Megan have made a list for how to be popular when they'd never once talked about what it really meant? "It means that everybody likes you," she said. "Everybody wants to be your friend."

"Everybody?" said Grams with a lift of her eyebrows. "That's a lot of people."

"And it means . . . it means you're the boss, sort of. You get to make the rules and everybody has to do what you say."

Grams's forehead wrinkled. "A big responsibility," she said.

"You have to wear really cool stuff, like the latest jeans. And your hair has to be perfect. And you have to smile all the time."

"I'm sure I couldn't do all that," said Grams. "I'd be exhausted!"

"And . . . Well, I guess that's it. Pretty much."

Grams nodded her head thoughtfully. "That's a lot to remember."

"You don't have to remember it, Grams. It's not for old—I mean, *older* people."

Grams grinned. "That's a relief! I don't like being nice all the time. And my hair! I can't do a thing with it."

"Oh, Grams," said Lucy.

"Oh, Luz," said Grams.

From a distance came the thin, high screech of a hawk. "Redtail," said Grams.

"Oh!" said Lucy, sitting up straight. She'd caught a glimpse of red in the rocks below. "I saw something!"

"Did you?" Her grandmother got to her feet. "Let's get closer."

Halfway down, the trail got narrower and the weeds taller, as tall as Grams. There were places where they had to hold the weeds back in order to push through.

"Watch your step," said Grams. By the time they were in the clear, they were standing just above the rocks. "We may be too close," she whispered. "Let's hunker down."

When they were quiet, Lucy could hear what was living all around them, lizards and crickets, things that darted and clicked. The weeds smelled like licorice and honey, and beneath that smell was another.

"I smell foxes," Lucy whispered. "I think."

Grams sniffed. "I've lost my sense of smell, I'm afraid. You'll have to be our nose."

She took off her straw hat. Shielding her eyes with her hand, she looked up, squinting. "What a day!"

For a long time, they watched the rocks where they thought a den might be. Out on the lake, two kayaks glided past. Lucy waved but the people didn't see her, or didn't want to stop paddling long enough to wave back.

Grams made a resting place by flattening down the weeds and lay back with her eyes already closed.

Lucy kept watch. She wanted so badly to see those fox kittens. *That* would be something to tell Megan.

Then, even though she didn't want to, she thought about Eddie. *He* was the one who loved kittens, any kind of kittens. She had helped him fill a scrapbook with pictures of cats and kittens cut out of magazines.

Grams began to snore, soft snuffling little snores. In the sunlight her face looked like crinkled-up paper. Her hair shone silver. A bee circled Grams's head and Lucy waved it away.

Below, a blue heron stepped carefully along the lake's edge as if it didn't want to get its feet wet.

Grams awoke with a snort and sat up. She put on her straw hat. "Any sign of the foxes?"

"Nope."

"I had a funny little dream about some friends I had when I was a child," said Grams. "We were trying to dig our way to India." She looked over at Lucy. "How's your friend Eddie? You spent a lot of time with him this summer."

"That was a job, Grams," said Lucy. "Eddie's not my friend."

"Oh?"

"Eddie's not . . ." She searched for the words she was supposed to use for Eddie. "He has Down syndrome. He has special needs."

"I see. Doesn't he need friends?"

Lucy thought about that. Of course Eddie needed friends. He probably thought that Lucy was a friend. But she wasn't. "I don't know," she said. She didn't want to think about Eddie anymore. That part of the summer was over. The job she thought of as Eddie was over. "I'm hungry. Let's climb back up to that rock and have our lunch."

Lucy led the way to the top, where they ate their turkey sandwiches and drank water.

Grams frowned at her sandwich. "Erika forgot to bring turkey. This is the last of it."

"When is she coming again?"

"Tomorrow."

"Ugh."

"I know, darling."

"Maybe she could, you know, stick her head in and then leave again. That would count."

Grams smiled. "Well, she's bringing groceries on Thursday and we'll want her to do that."

"I guess," said Lucy. "But she wouldn't have to stay."

Grams put the plastic bottle and sandwich baggies into her pack. "I suppose we'd better head back," she said. "The wind has come up a bit."

They crossed the lake with the wind at their backs and bumped up onto the shore.

Grams climbed out first. "That was easy," she said. "You don't always get a tailwind. We got lucky."

"But we didn't see the foxes," said Lucy.

"Not this time," said her grandmother. "But life is filled with surprises. I'm sure we'll have a few before the week is over."

Eddie kicked through the Matchbox cars on his floor. Without Lucy to play with, nothing in his room was any fun. He didn't want to draw or color or do a puzzle or read about Diego or Dora. He didn't want to do anything but sulk.

He went to find his mother. Sometimes she thought up things to do that were fun, but mostly she just took him shopping.

His mother was in the kitchen unloading the dishwasher. "There you are," she said. "How about giving me a hand?"

Eddie didn't like that expression. He knew his mother didn't really mean for him to take off his hand and give it to her. She explained all that to him once. But he still didn't like it. He began passing her glasses and plates, which she stacked neatly in the cupboard.

"Tyler's coming over today," his mother said. "Did you remember?"

Eddie shook his head. He did remember, but he

hadn't wanted to. Tyler's mother was Eddie's mother's friend, so Tyler and Eddie were supposed to be friends, too. But they were not. While their mothers drank coffee and talked and talked, he and Tyler pretended to get along.

Well, Eddie pretended. Tyler just punched letters into his phone or played his video game. If Eddie asked him a question, Tyler pretended not to hear it. What fun was that?

His mother closed the dishwasher. "Would you like to help me make some chocolate cupcakes? I know Tyler likes chocolate."

"I'll lick the bowl," Eddie said.

He went out the back door and called Doofus, the Ellerbys' big shaggy dog.

Doofus came tearing across the torn-up backyard and jumped against the fence that separated the Ellerbys from the Munches. He panted a hello with his big red tongue hanging out. Eddie hugged Doofus, while Doofus tried to lick Eddie's ear.

Doofus was lonely, too, Eddie could tell. And he was tired of playing in his yard. He had only one chew toy, a rubber bone.

Mrs. Ellerby came out her door carrying a trash can. "Hi, Eddie."

"Hi, Mrs. Ellerby."

"Doofus needs a bath," she said. "I'm going to give him one this afternoon."

"Can I help?"

"Sure. You can help hold on to him. He doesn't like to take baths."

"Can I take Doofus for a walk?"

"I guess you may. But you'd better ask your mother if it's all right."

Eddie ran into the house. "Mom! Mrs. Ellerby said I can take Doofus for a walk!"

Eddie's mother frowned. "Oh, I don't know," she said. "He's an awfully big dog."

"I can do it! Doofus likes me!"

His mother looked at the clock. "Tyler's coming in an hour," she said. "Ask Mrs. Ellerby if you can walk the dog later on."

"But I want to walk him now!"

"Eddie," his mother said in her warning voice.

"Okay, later on," said Eddie, and slammed out the door to tell Mrs. Ellerby.

✳

Waiting for Tyler, Eddie ate one of the cupcakes. Then, when his mother wasn't looking, he sneaked another and gobbled it down. The doorbell rang just as he was wiping a smear of frosting off his nose.

His mother came into the kitchen with Tyler and his mother. Tyler's mother was wearing jeans and cowboy boots. Her hair was in a ponytail. Tyler was wearing his baseball uniform.

"Tyler caught the ball for the final out!" his mother said.

"Terrific!" said Eddie's mother. "Why don't you and Eddie go play in Eddie's room. Eddie's got a new game." She turned to Tyler's mother. "Coffee, Angela?"

"Love some!" said Tyler's mother.

Tyler scowled.

"Go on now," his mother said, giving him a little push.

"So what's the game?" said Tyler when they were in Eddie's room.

"Chutes and Ladders," said Eddie. He went to his bookcase and took down the game.

"That's a baby game," said Tyler.

"No, it isn't." Was Tyler right? "We could play it."

"No, thanks," said Tyler. "I'm gifted and talented."

"What's that?"

"It's a special program for smart kids," said Tyler. He flopped down on Eddie's bed with his shoes on and took out his video game.

"My friend Lucy is very smart," said Eddie, but Tyler was no longer listening. It was almost like he was in a different room, or they had a fence between them like the Ellerbys and the Munches.

Eddie looked out his window at the grassy backyard. When his father came to visit, he always cut the grass and trimmed the bushes. Eddie would love having a dog like Doofus, even if he dug holes in the grass. The dog would be his friend, a friend that wouldn't know how to play video games.

It felt like three days before his mother stuck her head in to say it was time for Tyler to go home.

Tyler left without a word.

"Make sure to show him who's boss," said Mrs. Ellerby, clicking a leash to Doofus's collar. "He'll want to take you all over the place."

Eddie's mother had made him promise to only go around the block. That way he wouldn't have to cross any streets. Eddie could tell that she didn't know much about dogs. Dogs wanted to explore.

They set off down the sidewalk, Doofus pulling Eddie behind him. When they got to the end of the block, Doofus would have crossed without looking both ways if Eddie hadn't pulled him back. He was glad that he was strong. He had to do what Mrs. Ellerby said: show Doofus who was the boss.

"Come on, Doofus," he said, yanking Doofus into a left turn.

Doofus stopped a hundred times to smell things, grass and dirt and tree trunks. When a lady came by walking a tall skinny dog with hardly any hair, the two dogs stopped to smell each other's rear ends.

"Come, Hannah!" said the lady, and pulled her dog away. Doofus watched Hannah the dog leave as if he was in love.

Eddie liked walking Doofus. It was easy being Doofus's boss.

They were almost to the end of the block when Eddie heard a clatter. He turned and saw a gray cat come streaking out of someone's yard.

Doofus was gone in a flash. He bounded after the cat, his red leash dragging behind him.

"Doofus! Come back!" yelled Eddie. He took off, nearly stepping into the street before he remembered to look both ways. A car passed, then another, and by that time Doofus was gone.

Hot tears crowded Eddie's throat. What should he do? Go back and tell his mother? Mrs. Ellerby? Would they call the police? His first time walking a dog and he had blown it.

He wished he could call Lucy. She would come and help him find Doofus. She would tell him not to give up, that he gave up too easily.

Well, he wouldn't give up. He would find Doofus if it took all day.

Calling and calling, he walked three blocks, carefully crossing every street. At the end of a block, he followed some dog tracks that went left. They were too small to be Doofus's but he followed them anyway, keeping his head down like a good detective. Then the tracks disappeared and when he looked up he was at the dog-bus station. There were the shiny silver dog buses lined up to leave.

Eddie's father had come on the bus once, when his car broke. He said he would take Eddie on a bus ride "one of these days." But it was just like with his mother, one of these days never came. And when Lucy brought him here it was just to watch.

Eddie was staring at the buses when he felt something cold poking his hand.

"Doofus!" Eddie knelt and hugged the smelly dog. "You came back! Good boy!"

Eddie stood and wrapped Doofus's leash twice around his hand. "I'm the boss, Doofus," he said. "You have to do what I say."

Doofus looked up at Eddie with happy eyes, his tail wagging like anything.

"Okay," said Eddie. "We're going to go over to that bench and we're going to watch three buses leave, and then we have to go home and no arguments."

Eddie sat petting Doofus's head, which was resting on his knee. Doofus was fun. Pretty much fun. More fun than Tyler, that was for sure. But Eddie still missed Lucy. He missed her more than he liked chocolate cupcakes, way more. He sat watching the buses come and go and thought of Lucy, and then he began making his plan.

14

Grams took a catnap while Lucy worked a Sudoku puzzle. It was the diabolical kind, and after a while she gave up on it. She sat quietly and listened for Wild Thing. Sometimes, if he thought it was safe, the big gray tom would come to the door and stretch against the screen to be let in.

Grams said that Lucy was Wild Thing's favorite person because he had actually slept one whole night the summer before on Lucy's feet. Lucy hoped he would do that again. She missed Waldo, who considered Lucy his personal property and hated the outdoors as much as Wild Thing loved it.

Grams sat up. Her hair had come loose from the ponytail and hung down the sides of her face. "What day is it?" she said.

"Sunday!" How could her grandmother forget what day it was? She must have been dreaming.

"Yes, of course," said Grams. "I knew that." She stood and padded across the room in her bare feet and went outside. When she came back, she had in her hand the clay-streaked shirt that had once been Lucy's grand-father's. "Feel like working at the wheel a bit?"

Lucy's heart dropped like a stone to the bottom of the lake. She had known this was coming, and she knew she would give in, but it was the only part of staying with Grams she didn't enjoy. Throwing pots was harder than it looked, way harder. She hoped Grams didn't remember as clearly as she did the time, two summers ago, when Lucy in a fit of temper had smashed the lopsided pot she had almost pulled up.

Forgetting would not be such a bad thing, she de-cided, if all you forgot were the unpleasant things, the times people hurt your feelings or lost their temper at something that wasn't even your fault.

"I'll make a coil pot," said Lucy, reaching for the shirt.

"Yes, good practice. Then you can try the wheel again."

Why was it so important to Grams that she learn to throw a stupid pot?

She followed her grandmother out the back door and across the yard to the old pottery shed. The dirt all around was raked bare. Some distance from the wooden shed was Grams's brick kiln, where she fired her pots. Af-ter they were glazed and fired again, she would take them down to a gallery, where they sold for hundreds of dollars.

Now and then people would find their way to Grams's house, asking politely or sometimes not too politely if they could watch her work. Once it was a woman from an art magazine. She had taken photographs of Grams at work and now the magazine lay somewhere in the pile by the side of the sofa. Grams wasn't half so proud of it as Lucy was.

From the corner of her eye, Lucy watched her grandmother pulling up a pot, her knobby right hand going from a bowl of water to the clay, the creak of the old wheel the only sound. Lucy figured if she rolled her clay snakes very quietly, her grandmother might just forget she was there.

No such luck. Her grandmother ran a wire under the tall cylinder she'd made and lifted the pot from the wheel. "Ready to give it a try?"

From out of Lucy came the sigh that was so like her mother's and her grandmother's. "Okay."

Lucy climbed onto the bench and sat with slumped shoulders, waiting.

"You look as if you're going to the guillotine," Grams said, laughing. "You don't have to do this if you really don't want to."

But she couldn't bear to disappoint her grandmother. "No, it's okay. It's just that I'm so awful at it."

"It isn't easy. You're not awful. You're learning. There's a difference." She set a ball of clay in front of Lucy and gave the wheel a kick to get her started.

In the art magazine, the writer had made a big deal about the fact that Luz Ortega still used an old-fashioned kick wheel. An electric one would help her turn out pots more quickly and easily, she said. Especially when you considered the potter's "advanced age."

Maybe that was why Grams didn't like that article and had just tossed the magazine onto the pile.

"I'll put my hands over yours and we'll do it together."

Grams's warm breath tickled Lucy's neck and a lock of hair whispered against her ear. "Ready?"

Lucy nodded. The clay beneath her cupped hands was slick and, after a little while of turning under their hands, as smooth as chocolate pudding.

"Feel that?" said Grams. "That stillness?"

Lucy concentrated. All she could feel was a wet ball of spinning mud. "Nope."

"Close your eyes."

Lucy closed her eyes, but nothing changed.

"There," said Grams. "The pot is centered. Now you can start to pull it up."

Lucy expected Grams to let go, which was when the trouble began before. But she didn't. A small bowl began to form as Grams's fingers pulled the clay and Lucy's fingers up from the base. All she told Lucy was not to pinch too hard.

"There! How's that?" said Grams, lifting her hands.

It was perfect, a perfect little bowl. "It can be for Wild Thing," said Lucy. "A new cat bowl."

But then she had another thought. She would take it home and show Megan that she, too, was an artist.

With her hands on her hips, Grams looked down at the lake, glimmering silver through the trees. "How about a swim?" she said.

Lucy thought for a moment. "Won't the water be cold?"

"Oh, yes," said Grams. "That's the fun part."

They changed into their suits and, wrapped in towels, made their way down to the lake.

At the water's edge, Lucy dipped her toe in. "It's cold!" She pulled the towel more tightly around her shoulders.

Grams dropped her towel and waded right in. "Last one in's a rotten egg!" she cried. Lifting her arms, she dove. Lucy could see her wavering shape moving through the water.

At last her grandmother came up. "It's perfect!" she said.

Lucy dropped her towel. The water surrounding her ankles, then her knees and inching up her thighs felt icy. She wanted badly to back out. But there was her grandmother being so brave and laughing at her granddaughter, who couldn't even put her belly in. Then Grams started a splashing contest and Lucy dove. She popped up laughing.

Treading water, she turned and looked all around her. Cold or not, she was right where she needed to be. With her Grams, in the water, just like all the summers before. Right this moment, Lucy was as happy as she'd ever been in her life.

"Thanks, Grams," she said.

Her grandmother, floating on her back like a stick, lifted her head. "What for?"

"For everything!" said Lucy. "For making me so happy."

"Oh, that's easy," said Grams, laying her head back and closing her eyes. "You do it all yourself, you know."

15

The first thing Lucy thought about when she opened her eyes in the morning was her lost bracelet. Then Megan. Then her birthday when Megan gave it to her. She had clasped the beautiful gold bracelet on Lucy's wrist, turning it round and round so they could admire it together.

"See?" Megan had said. "It's a circle that never ends. Just like our friendship." Megan would be devastated if she knew that Lucy no longer had the bracelet. She would think Lucy didn't care about it. But she did! The bracelet meant everything to her.

Maybe she could buy another one just like it. But something about that felt very wrong. Every time she looked at the tiny golden hearts she would feel like a cheat.

Lucy sat up. Someone was burning leaves. She looked out through the dusty screen. Treetops in a clear blue sky, as if they were sailing across it. No smoke. She sniffed again. It was coming from inside the house.

Bolting from the bed, she ran into the kitchen and stopped dead. Before her eyes, a line of orange flame was snaking its way from the stove straight up the wall.

"Grams!"

Lucy grabbed the biggest pot she could find. Sticking it under the faucet, she yelled for her grandmother again. Flames licked the bottom of the cupboard. When the pot was half full, Lucy dashed the water on the fire. It sputtered and went out, leaving a black trail of soot up the wall. Smoke drifted into the ceiling.

Her heart beating wildly, Lucy pulled the charred dish towel, still smoldering, across the stove and into the sink.

She had not been watching. She had been told to be extra cautious and she hadn't been. Her knees felt rubbery.

What if she hadn't been here at all? What might have happened to her grandmother then?

Lucy went to the back door, cupped her hand against the screen, and peered out. "Grams?"

Grams stood up, a hand on her lower back. A trail of dry cat kibble ran from the edge of the woods up to the steps. "Hi, Lucy. I suppose this is useless. The raccoons will eat it before Wild Thing comes around."

"Didn't you hear me calling you?" Lucy's voice trembled with fear. Her heart bumped around in her chest, looking for a way out.

"I didn't hear you. What is it?"

Lucy bit her lip. She should have cleaned up the mess.

But there was no hiding it. The wall would have to be repaired, at least painted.

"There was a fire," she said. "On the stove. But it's out now."

"Oh, dear!" said Grams. Her hands dropped to her sides, and for a second she looked afraid.

"It's okay, Grams," said Lucy quickly. "I caught it in time."

Her grandmother came inside. She stopped in front of the stove. Then she turned away and went straight into the bathroom.

Lucy waited. The bathroom was the only place in the house where you could be alone if you needed to be. But why did her grandmother need to be alone? It wasn't like her.

When she came out, her eyes were red-rimmed. Had she been crying? Grams?

"Will you make us a cup of tea, Lucy?" she said. "I'm awfully angry at that stove right now."

Lucy almost blurted that it wasn't the stove's fault, which is what she'd have said at home had the same thing happened there.

But it wouldn't have happened at home. It happened here, and only because her grandmother had left the towel too close to the burner and gone outside with the burner left on.

Lucy wrung out the ruined dish towel and slipped it into the trash can under the sink. She filled the teakettle and lit the stove.

Her grandmother had begun placing logs in the fireplace, the way she did every afternoon. Only it was still morning. Lucy wanted to stop her, tell her that they didn't need a fire. Not tonight.

But they did. Lucy did. She couldn't imagine her day ending without a curl-up on the sofa with Grams in front of a roaring fire.

But this time she would keep watch.

Eddie went to the window and watched his mother back the car into the street.

Before she left, she had reminded him that it was Monday. She had two appointments on Monday. One with the doctor and one with the dentist.

She had told him to be careful.

She had told him to be good.

She said she would be gone for a couple of hours and that he was in charge.

He should not answer the telephone.

If he got hungry, he should eat his snack slowly.

If he got sleepy, he should take a nap.

He should keep the front door locked.

There were more things, but Eddie could not remember them all.

He went to his dresser and pulled out a drawer.

Inside were his clothes, neatly folded.

He took out some underwear and ten pairs of rolled-up socks.

In the second drawer lay all his T-shirts. He took out his favorite Mickey Mouse Disneyland shirt, his second favorite, a polar bear shirt, and another shirt with big dinosaurs on it. He would wear that one to scare the bad guys away.

He decided not to think anymore about the bad guys. Maybe they weren't even real, and were only on TV.

His striped pj's were in the bottom drawer, and he took those out as well.

Then he opened his red backpack and tried to stuff all the clothes inside. But the zipper wouldn't close. His clothes were still popping out.

He dumped everything onto the floor.

Would he really need all his school supplies? He didn't think so. But just in case, he put in the pens.

Back into the pack went his T-shirts, pj's, two undershorts, a pair of shorts, and the ten pairs of socks.

Last of all, he carefully put Lucy's bracelet into the zipper compartment, where it would be safe.

Then he sat on his bed to think.

Some things he knew: telling his mother where he was going was not a good idea; taking the dog bus cost money; Lucy went to the lake, and Lucy would be missing him.

He knew this because of how he felt inside, missing her.

He got down on his knees and lifted the blanket to look under his bed. It was dark under there. At first all he saw were books and cars. The dust bunnies made him sneeze three times.

Then he saw his bank, a pig made out of plastic. You could see right through it to the money.

He pulled the pig out and shook it upside down, but nothing fell from the slit in the top. He shook it again, this time harder. Still nothing.

He put the bank down and told the pig that he was sorry but that he had to get his money.

Then he stood, took one big deep breath, and jumped on the pig with both feet. *Crack* went the pig, and out spilled the money.

He gathered the paper money and two fistfuls of coins and put it all into the pocket of his backpack.

Now a little clock was ticking very hard in his throat. He sat back down on his bed to think some more.

He didn't want to think about the time he got lost in the big store, but he couldn't help it. In the big store, his mother had disappeared and was gone a very long time. He thought she had gone to heaven, where his grandpa was, and wouldn't come back for him, so he climbed under a rack of soft lady nighties where the bogeyman couldn't get him.

When his mother found him, she was very upset. She made him say his address a million times.

Then she bought him an ice cream.

"Two forty-two Fortuna Street, Goleta, California," he said, just like he said then. "Two forty-two Fortuna Street, Goleta, California." He could write it now because of Lucy.

He looked at his and Lucy's house pictures on the

wall. Then he walked across his SpongeBob rug and took them down. Folding them like his mother had taught him to fold napkins, he put them into his backpack.

He didn't break one rule.

Snack.

He went into the kitchen and opened the fridge, and there it was waiting: graham crackers with peanut butter on them. He took one bite and put the rest into a little baggie. He zipped up the baggie and put it into his backpack. When he was hungry, he would eat the snack, slowly like his mother said.

He struggled to put on his backpack that jingled and jangled as he crossed the living room. At the door his hand went up to the lock. Then his hand went down. "Keep the front door locked," his mother had said.

He went to the couch to sit and think.

Three times he went back to the door, each time raising his hand and watching it fall again. His chest kept grinding as if it had teeth. If he couldn't unlock the door, he couldn't go to the dog-bus station and he couldn't get to the lake.

An idea bright as the sun popped into his head: back door. "Easy as that," Miss Salgado, his teacher, always said. "Easy as that." His heart beating *thumpity-thump*, he hurried through the living room, across the black-and-white tiles of the kitchen, and out the back door into the yard.

Whew!

Doofus jumped up on his side of the fence. His tail

went back and forth, back and forth, like a windshield wiper.

"Hi, Doofus! Hi, Doofus!" Eddie patted Doofus on the head. Doofus shook all over because he was so happy.

Then Eddie leaned down and Doofus washed his face with his long pink tongue. Now he was clean and ready to go.

"See you later, Doofus!"

But Doofus couldn't give the alligator answer because he was only a dog.

"Hi, whirlies," he said, crossing his front yard. "Bye, whirlies."

They couldn't talk either, but they all waved goodbye.

17

"Ah, here she comes now," said Grams from the door. "Only a little late."

Lucy watched the girl named Erika coming up the drive on foot. She was big. Not fat, but tall, with shoulders like a football player's. Her hair hung down in greasy-looking strings.

"Hello, Erika," said Grams, stepping back to let the big girl pass. "This is my granddaughter, Luz."

Erika glanced at Lucy with dull eyes. "Hello," she said.

"Hi," said Lucy, suddenly shy. She'd already planned how to act, what to say when the *other* Erika came, the one she'd imagined when she'd heard a sixteen-year-old girl was coming. A girl not exactly gorgeous, which would be way too intimidating, but pretty and really, really nice.

If she remembered right, "Always be complimentary" was number four on the top tips list. Lucy's brain searched for something nice to say about Erika's outfit.

"I like your T-shirt," she said at last.

She didn't really like it at all. The shirt was black and had a rock group on it with a name that Lucy had never heard of, Slither Soup.

Erika looked at Lucy as if she could read her mind. "You know this group?"

"Um, no," said Lucy.

"My boyfriend's in it," said Erika. "He gave me this." She stuck out her right hand. On one stubby finger was a tarnished silver ring with a cross on it.

Lucy thought about her beautiful bracelet with the golden hearts. "Oh," she said. "Nice."

"The furniture could use a good dusting, dear," said Grams. "And there's a little bit of smudge on the wall over the stove." She glanced quickly at Lucy. "Lucy and I will be out in the potting shed if you need anything."

"Sure," said Erika, with a shrug.

Lucy followed Grams out to the shed.

"She's a sweet girl underneath," said Grams. "But a little mixed up, I think. Here, stir this, will you?" She handed Lucy a wooden spoon and Lucy began to pull it through the thick glaze.

Grams took a bisque-fired pot from the shelf. "Would you like to glaze this one?"

"Okay. Sure. What color?"

"Imagine how you'd like it to look. What colors you'd like to use, and what design."

Lucy tried to imagine the finished pot, but all she could see was the kind of pot her grandmother always made using colors of the earth and sky. "Um, blue I guess. Mostly blue. With some brown, um . . . bears!" The summer before, a black bear had been captured in Grams's backyard. Now Grams's trash cans had locks on them.

"Blue with bears," said Grams. "I think we can do that."

Lucy did the work herself, with only a little help from Grams. She could hardly wait for the pot to be fired. Maybe it would sell along with her grandmother's pots, for hundreds of dollars.

Glazing was fun. It was throwing she didn't like.

"Let's take these out to the kiln," said Grams when eight pots, including Lucy's, were lined up on the worktable.

They took the pots two at a time out to the kiln and set them carefully on the shelves inside. Then Lucy helped Grams brick up the kiln and fire it.

"That's a good day's work," said Grams. "Let's go inside and see what we have for lunch."

Sitting at the table, Erika was playing with her greasy hair and thumbing through one of Megan's magazines. Her fingernails were broken and dirty.

Lucy could only imagine what Megan would have to say about Erika and Erika's chances for popularity. She wondered if Erika ever washed her hair. Or her face, which was covered with angry-looking spots and bumps.

Maybe she'd get some ideas for a makeover from the magazine.

"I finished the dusting but the wall won't come clean," Erika said, looking up. "Can I go now?"

"I'll make you a grocery list," said Grams. When she was finished, she handed it to Erika. "You forgot the turkey last time, dear. And the cleanser, too. The one in the green can."

Erika looked down at the list. "Oh," she said. "Sorry. It's your writing."

But Grams's writing was beautiful! She still wrote to Lucy the old-fashioned way, by snail mail, and all the letters were perfectly formed. Penmanship had been a big thing when Grams was a girl, and Grams had won prizes for hers.

"I'll print it for you, then," said Grams. She took back the list and made another.

"She's an unhappy girl," said Grams as they watched Erika slouch down the hill.

"She's probably not popular," Lucy said with a sigh.

Eddie wandered up to the end of his block. Looking both ways two times, he crossed the street.

"Two forty-two Fortuna Street, Goleta, California," he said over and over to himself, until it became a nursery rhyme. "Two forty-two Fortuna Street, Goleta, California."

A lady with a bouncing tail of hair and a red visor ran past, pushing a baby stroller. "Hi!" he said, but she didn't answer. He liked babies more than people. Babies smiled at you and looked you right in the eyes. Some babies stunk like a skunk but that was okay. They couldn't help it.

Sometimes he asked his mother for a baby, but she always said no. She was too old, she said. He told her he would feed the baby and hold it and take it for walks, but still she said no. Not even "maybe sometime." Just no.

Next time his father came for a weekend, he would

ask him for a baby. Fathers didn't make babies in their stomachs, but his father could buy a baby instead of the new bike he had promised Eddie for his birthday.

He stopped in front of a white house with blue trim and an orange kitty in the yard.

"Here kitty kitty," he said, kneeling down on the grass. But the kitty just stared with its big yellow eyes.

Eddie got up and brushed the grass off his knees.

At the next street he remembered to look both ways, and crossed.

Yelling, a boy on a bike pedaled past him on the sidewalk. "Outta my way! Outta my way!"

Eddie leaped sideways, tripping over a string fence and landing in a heap on the soft dirt.

A witch popped her head out of the house window. "Get off my seeds!" she shrieked.

Eddie held his ears. He looked around. More seeds. How could he get up without touching any seeds? But when the door opened, he didn't worry about the seeds anymore. He got up as fast as he could and took off running.

Breathless, he stopped and turned around. He'd crossed another street without looking both ways. That was a rule and he'd broken it.

Looking both ways twice, he recrossed the same street.

Then, looking both ways twice, he crossed it again.

This was his favorite block because it had way tall peely-bark trees with little hard nuggets that smelled like peppermint gum. He picked a few off the ground and zipped them into the pouch of his backpack along with his money and Lucy's golden heart bracelet.

He crossed the next street after looking both ways twice and then waiting for two cars to pass.

Where was the bus station? He knew it wasn't behind him and it wasn't in front of him because he had already counted four blocks.

Left or right?

He turned to the left, shading his eyes to see as far as an eagle. No dog buses.

He turned to the right and, like magic, there they were. The buses were there all the time! Heart dancing, he began to jog, his backpack bouncing and jingling, sweat running down the sides of his face.

The dog buses stunk more than babies. Covering his nose and mouth with his hands, he went to the line where people waited to buy their tickets. All of him sweaty now, he was starting to stink worse than the babies, worse than the buses. When he got to the lake, he would wash off all the sweat in the blue water.

The three people ahead of him got their tickets and then it was Eddie's turn. He could hear the buses behind him leaving and it made him anxious. What if one of those buses was going to the lake?

He began to chew on his tongue.

"Where to, young fella?" said the ticket man.

"Two forty-two Fortuna Street, Goleta, California," said Eddie. But right away he knew that was wrong.

"Up the street," said the ticket man, pointing.

"No!" said Eddie. "I'm going to the lake."

The ticket man frowned. "Which lake is that? What city?"

Eddie shrugged off his pack and set it on the ground. It rolled over and he set it up again. Unzipping it, he took out his pictures.

A deep voice behind him said, "Hey, we ain't got all day," making him jump.

Eddie stood with his pack unzipped and gave Lucy's lake picture to the ticket man.

"Crescent Lake," read the ticket man. "That'll be twenty-four dollars and eighty cents. Are you sure you know where you're going?"

"Yup," said Eddie, giving the ticket man all his paper money. "Crescent Lake."

"Is there somebody there to meet you?"

"Lucy," said Eddie.

The ticket man shrugged. "Okay," he said, the way his mother said okay when she wasn't really sure. Then the ticket man pushed a white ticket, some paper money, and two coins under the window.

Eddie clutched the ticket and the money in his sweaty hand.

He went to the waiting bench where he and Lucy always sat.

He zipped up his pack.

It wasn't a very long wait. A big, shiny silver dog bus came driving off the highway right into the station. Eddie hopped up and ran to the door, first in line.

The door folded open.

Eddie climbed up the steps.

He held out his ticket.

The driver glanced at it. "Wrong bus," he said.

Eddie stood in the little space between the driver and the steps until the driver said to let the other people in.

When all the people were on, Eddie got off. With a big lump in his throat he waved to the bus as it left.

Back to the bench to wait some more.

Three times he got up and ran to the bus and three times he went back to the bench.

The fourth driver glanced at his ticket and pushed it into a slot.

Eddie waited.

"Move it, bro," said a voice behind him, so Eddie went down the aisle until he found a seat by the window where he sat hugging his pack and shaking all over. The teeth in his chest were gone. Now there were gnats, which wasn't so bad, but he had to keep swallowing so they would stay down and not come flying out of his mouth, and now he was thirsty.

A man with black skin and fuzzy hair swung into the seat beside him. There were white wires coming out of his ears. His head bounced on his long black neck and his eyes were closed. His shirt had orange-and-yellow splashes and a big green leaf in the middle that looked like a hand.

The bus made a whooshing sound and began to move. Eddie got a scary thought that he should jump up and run out of the bus before it was too late, but he swallowed the thought down.

He closed his eyes like the black-skinned man, but it

was darker and scarier in there than it was on the bus, so he opened his eyes and watched the world going by the window, trees and houses, cars and more cars, big loud trucks, a red sign with the big yellow M, and after a while he fell asleep.

"Yo!" said a voice.

Eddie opened his eyes. His head lay sideways. Spit trickled out of his mouth. The black-skinned man's face was frowning down at him. Eddie could see now that his skin wasn't really black. It was dark brown, the color of chocolate.

"You're sloppin' all over me, child! Stay in your own seat now."

Eddie sat up straight. He felt dizzy and a little sick until he remembered where he was.

"Where y'all goin'?" said the chocolate man.

"To see Lucy," said Eddie.

"She your girlfriend?"

Eddie thought. "She's a girl and she's my friend," he said. "She's been gone for two whole days."

The chocolate man was quiet for a little bit. Then he said, "You're one of them slow folks, right?"

Eddie thought about that. It was true that he always came in last in the races at his school. His feet were too big for running.

"Yes," he said.

"Thought so," said the man. "Let me tell you something."

"Okay."

The chocolate man frowned. "You shouldn't go talking to no strangers, you hear?"

"I can hear," said Eddie.

"You listen to me then. Strangers coming up to you asking for money and like that? You walk right away or you call the cops come and get 'em, hear?"

"I hear," said Eddie.

"All right then," said the chocolate man.

"All right then," said Eddie.

"And another thing. People call you a dummy and such like? You tell 'em right off, 'I ain't no dummy.' Hear?"

"I hear," said Eddie.

"Lemme hear you say it then."

"I ain't no dummy," said Eddie.

"Nah! You say it like you's afraid of your own shadow. Say it loud. I AIN'T NO DUMMY!"

A man in the seat in front of them turned around and stared at them through his glittery glasses.

Eddie squeaked in his littlest voice, "I ain't no dummy."

"Now you's whisperin'," said the chocolate man. "You gotta practice that, hear?"

"I hear," said Eddie.

Was the chocolate man a stranger? He didn't ask for anything. He gave Eddie something. A rule. Two rules. So he wasn't a stranger, but his eyes had closed again, so Eddie couldn't talk to him even if he wanted to. Which he sort of did and sort of didn't.

He unzipped his pack. He checked to see that Lucy's

bracelet was still there. Then he took out his snack. It wasn't a very big snack and he was very hungry, but he ate it slowly just like he was supposed to.

After the last bite, his mouth was stuck together. He didn't have his milk to wash the sticky down.

He tapped the chocolate man on the shoulder.

"Yo," said the chocolate man.

Eddie tapped his shoulder again.

The chocolate man's eyes opened.

"I need a drink," said Eddie.

"I hear that," said the chocolate man. "They don't serve no drinks on this bus. 'Sides, you're too young to drink."

"No I'm not. I'm thirteen. I drink all sorts of things. Every day."

The chocolate man sighed. He shook his head and sort of laughed. "Back of the bus," he said, with his thumb pointing backward. "Get you some water in the head."

Eddie went down the aisle, clutching seats as he went. He wondered which head the black-skinned man meant. There were two heads to every seat.

"Excuse me," he said to a boy in a baseball cap. "I need to find the head with the water."

"It's there," said the boy, pointing.

"Where?" said Eddie.

"There, dummy! Right there. That door."

"I AIN'T NO DUMMY!" said Eddie.

The boy pulled the brim of his cap down over his eyes. A woman in the next seat smiled.

Eddie went to the door and pulled on the knob but

the door wouldn't open. He pulled and pulled until another lady got up out of her seat and showed him how the knob had to go sideways first.

Behind the door was a little bathroom. Eddie stepped inside and turned on the water in the little sink. Cupping his hands under the tiny faucet, he drank and drank until his stomach felt like a water balloon. The water sloshed around in there all the way back to his seat.

19

Lucy and Grams walked arm in arm along the lake. The afternoon was cool and windy and the sky overcast. Grams had on the thin green cardigan that hung, when it wasn't being worn, from a hook by the back door. Lucy was snug in her Windbreaker. She found a feather and stuck it through the hole in the back of her Dodgers cap.

"Hawk's feather," said Grams. "You don't find those often. They're good luck."

Lucy searched for more feathers. She picked up tiny pinecones and interesting pebbles, putting them into her pockets until they were weighted down.

"Let's take a little rest, shall we?" Grams said when they'd come to one of the benches set above the lake. Hat Island lay in the distance, gray against the paler sky.

"I think I know what the problem is," said Grams.

"What problem?"

A sparrow landed at their feet and began searching the ground for bugs.

"With Erika. I think she can't read."

"She's probably a dropout," said Lucy. "She looks like a dropout."

The sparrow cocked its head and peered up at Lucy.

Her grandmother's gray eyebrows met over the rims of her glasses. Through the smudged lenses, she studied Lucy's face. "Is there a certain look, then?"

But Lucy had to admit she really didn't know. She'd been guessing, that's all. "She seems sort of stupid."

Immediately, she knew she'd said the wrong thing.

"Uneducated, yes, but not necessarily stupid," said Grams. "I prefer the word *ignorant* myself."

"That's just as bad."

"Not really. *Ignorant* simply means unlearned. Unenlightened."

Was Eddie ignorant? He wasn't stupid. And he was a heck of a lot nicer than Erika.

Lucy crossed her arms. "Well, it's pretty stupid to drop out of school, if you ask me."

"Oh, it is. Absolutely. I know that now, but not when I did it."

Lucy's mouth fell open. "You dropped out? Grams!"

A look of dismay came over Grams's face. "Oh, dear. That was one of the things I wasn't supposed to tell you." She laughed, but stopped when she saw the shock on Lucy's face. "You see, I was the only child left at home to support the younger ones. Times were hard then." Grams's smile was wistful. "Your mother, bless her heart, tried to convince me you'd only be harmed by all those old stories. But how can that be? One can learn from poor examples as well as good ones, don't you think?"

"You're not a poor example, Grams. You're the best example."

"Well, I *was* a dropout."

"Yes, but—"

"Just like Erika."

"Grams! I can't believe you would drop out of school!"

Grams took Lucy's hands in hers. "Oh, dear. Now I've upset you. Your mother was right."

"No!" Lucy cried. The sparrow, startled, leaped into flight. "My mother's never right!" She frowned. "Well, mostly never. I'm just . . . just surprised, that's all. I mean, you're so smart. How did you get so smart without going to school?"

Delight crept back into Grams's smile. "Well, I *was* sixteen when I left Garfield High. I'd learned a few things by then. And after that? Well, I've always been a voracious reader. You could say, I suppose, that I was my own teacher."

Lucy thought about homework, what a fight she always had with herself to get it done. "That sounds hard," she said.

"I didn't say it was easy," said Grams. "But nothing worthwhile ever is. Is it?"

Lucy thought about that for a while. She had the feeling that her grandmother was right, but she didn't want her to be. "Why can't things just be easy?"

"Good question," said Grams. "I'll have the answer on my hundredth birthday. How's that?"

"But I'll already be grown up!"

"Right. You'll be all grown up and then you can tell me."

They started back up the hill, Lucy kicking through the pine needles, thinking, thinking . . .

"Grams?"

"Luz?" Grams opened the screen door and Lucy followed her in.

"What else don't I know about you?"

Her grandmother turned, mischief in her eyes. Then something that looked like sadness passed through like a cloud over the sun. "You want to know secrets, do you?"

"Yes," said Lucy. "I'm twelve now, you know. If you'll tell me your secrets, I'll tell you mine."

"Deal," said Grams, and they shook on it.

When Eddie awoke again, the chocolate man was gone. In his place was a lady so big that she took up part of Eddie's seat. He craned his head around. Where was the chocolate man? He stood up, banging his head on the luggage rack. Rubbing his head, Eddie looked at every seat, but the chocolate man wasn't in any of them.

In his dream, the bus had stopped and some people got off and on.

Maybe it wasn't a dream. Maybe the chocolate man really did go away without saying goodbye.

A friend wouldn't do that. The chocolate man probably didn't want to wake Eddie up, that's all.

"Goodbye, chocolate man," he said.

The big lady, whose lipstick was colored outside the lines, stared at him through her sparkly glasses. "What did you say?"

"Goodbye, chocolate man," said Eddie. "He's my friend."

"Where is your mother?" she said.

"She's at the doctor's," said Eddie. "Or the dentist's." And suddenly he missed his mom like anything. His throat got hot. Hot tears drowned his eyeballs and slid down his cheeks and chin and onto his wrinkled-up T-shirt.

The big lady put her spotty hand on his wrist. Her red fingernails stuck out like bloody tiger claws. "Where are you going?"

She had a lullaby voice and her fingerpads were pillowy soft.

Eddie told her.

"I am disembarking in Pinehurst," she said. "That's where my grandchildren reside. Peter and Jenny. They're twins, don't you know."

Eddie said he didn't know. He rolled the *disembarking* word around in his mouth. It was a really big word. He would save it for Lucy.

"I am disembarking in Crescent Lake," he would say, and watch her eyes get big with surprise.

The big lady talked on and on like a teacher. Eddie wanted to look out the window. He didn't want to be impolite (his mother's word), but his eyes did. They kept sliding all the way over so they could see the cars and trucks and trees and houses and buildings passing by the window.

After a million years, the bus slowed and went down a big ramp. The bus driver stopped the bus by a green-and-white building and got out. On the back side of the building was a tall pole with the dog sign on it.

The big lady got up. "This is my stop," she said. "It's been very nice talking to you, young man. Don't forget to get off the bus in Crescent Lake."

"I won't forget," said Eddie. "Lucy is there."

Almost everybody on the bus got off, so Eddie did, too. He followed the bus driver into the green-and-white building.

A delicious smell went up his nose and filled his head like a sweet cloud.

Doughnuts. Zillions and zillions of doughnuts.

Down a rolling sidewalk thing came doughnuts with frosting melted on the top and dripping over the sides.

Some had chocolate sprinkles, some had colored sprinkles, some didn't have any holes, some had sugar dust, and some had red jelly oozing out.

Eddie held on to his fingers so they wouldn't grab one.

He stood for a very long time watching the doughnuts rolling along, then getting snatched up by a lady with pincers, who put them into the window case.

After a while he went over to the case. He walked up and down looking at every doughnut and trying to decide which one he would buy.

Red jelly. No! Chocolate sprinkles.

Did he have enough money for two?

He was kneeling down to count the money in his backpack when he heard the bus engine. He jumped up.

The dog bus was driving away! Without him!

He made a dash for the door, tripping over his pack and spilling his money. "Wait!"

Coins rolled in every direction.

Eddie didn't know what to do, grab his money or run for the bus.

These were two important things. How could he decide?

He stood at the door chewing on his tongue until the bus was out of sight and one decision gone.

He got down on his hands and knees and crawled around on the floor looking under every table and chair for his money. The zigzag floor made him dizzy.

When he was sure he'd gathered up every last coin, he put the money into his backpack and sat in one of the green plastic chairs to think.

He wasn't lost. He wasn't lost. When you're lost you don't know where you are and your mother is looking for you all over and crying. Eddie knew exactly where he was.

Then he didn't.

He tried to remember the name of the place where Peter and Jenny lived, but he couldn't.

He hugged his backpack. Birds were flying around all inside him, bumping against his red beating heart and the birdcage of his ribs with their sharp little beaks.

He needed an ice cream. But this was a doughnut store. He didn't want a doughnut anymore.

And then he did. He was very hungry. He'd only had one very teeny snack and some water.

He got up and went to the counter.

He looked through the rows of doughnuts in both cases.

He made up his mind and changed his mind.

He made up his mind for the very last time.

"One jelly doughnut," he told the doughnut girl. "And one chocolate sprinkle."

Whew!

He unzipped his pack and grabbed a fistful of coins.

"And milk," he said. "Pretty please with sugar on it."

The doughnut girl giggled. She pinched two doughnuts out of the window case and put each one into its own little baggie. She took a red-and-white box of milk out of the fridge and set it on the counter. "That'll be three dollars and eighty cents," she said.

Eddie scooped the rest of the money out of his pack and put the whole lot on the counter.

The doughnut girl began sorting through it. When she was finished, she pushed a pile of coins back to Eddie. "There you go," she said.

Eddie took the doughnuts and milk to his table and sat down to eat.

The doughnuts were melty good and delicious, but after a while they began to stick in his throat where the tears kept coming up. He kept swallowing the whole mess down with milk.

The doughnut machine had stopped. All the doughnuts were snug in their cases and no one came in to buy them. Poor lonesome doughnuts.

The doughnut girl had gone to sit at a table in the back. Chewing on the side of her thumb, she turned the pages of a magazine.

She had brown hair and brown eyes just like Lucy.

"Twofortytwofortunastreetgoletacalifornia," Eddie repeated over and over to himself until his address was one big smear.

Bus engine! Eddie jumped up, grabbed his backpack, and bolted for the door.

Outside. The dog bus driving in. Eddie turned back.

He opened the door to the doughnut store. "Goodbye!" he said to the doughnut girl. "I have to go now."

She lifted her head and smiled, waving the tops of her fingers.

The driver got off the bus. It was a different driver, a grandfather driver with gray hair and a gray mustache. A bunch of people got off the bus just like before.

Eddie ran to the bus. He climbed on. He sat in the very first seat, right behind the bus driver seat, holding his big fat baby of a backpack.

This time he would stay awake if he had to pinch himself a thousand times. He practiced on his arm until the grandfather bus driver came back.

The grandfather bus driver climbed up the steps and frowned down at Eddie. "Where did you come from?" he said in his deep grandfather voice.

"The doughnut store," said Eddie.

"Aha," said the grandfather bus driver. "And where are you going?"

Eddie rubbed the side of his thumb where the skin was wearing away. "Crescent Lake. I'm going to see Lucy."

"This bus doesn't stop in Crescent Lake," said the grandfather bus driver. "What's your ticket say?"

Eddie froze. His ticket was gone. It went on the bus with the other driver.

"I got off the bus," he said, real fast. "By mistake. The bus went away with my ticket."

The mean little pecking birds were back.

The grandfather bus driver looked at him under his gray eyebrows that were bushy and crawling across his forehead to meet each other. At last he said, "Okeydoke," the way his father said it when he came for a visit. Only his father said "okeydoke" to make Eddie laugh when he didn't really want to. "I guess we can make one unscheduled stop."

The grandfather bus driver sat down and started up the bus. People came hurrying out of the doughnut store and climbing up the steps. "Lordy!" said a smiley-faced chocolate lady with sugar powder on her face. "That was enough to bust my corset."

What was a corset? Was that another word for stomach? Now he had two words to remember, except he'd already forgotten the first one. He chased it around inside his brain for a while and finally gave up.

21

"Crescent Lake!"

Eddie opened his eyes. It was almost nighttime. His neck was stiff from leaning his head against the wall of the bus. Eddie stood up. His knees were stiff. His back felt crooked. Hugging his backpack, he went down the three steps and just like magic he was standing on the sidewalk of Crescent Lake.

"Bye!" he said, waving as the bus drove off.

The lake was not as blue as Lucy colored it. In the almost dark it was silvery black, and the sun was melting right into it like orange sherbet. He looked around. There were way too many houses. But not houses exactly. Boxes. Boxes on top of boxes. None of them looked like the house in Lucy's picture.

Eddie began to panic. He hopped from one foot to the other. He flapped his hands.

How would he ever find Lucy in Crescent Lake? It was big, really big.

"Two forty-two Fortuna Street Goleta California," he

said over and over. "Two forty-two Fortuna Street Goleta California."

He sat down on the curb and took out Lucy's bracelet. He counted the twelve tiny gold hearts. With the bracelet in his hand, he wasn't freaked. Scared, but not freaked.

Ice cream. He needed some ice cream. When he was scared, his mother always bought him ice cream.

He got up and walked a block, then another, looking for an ice cream store. Some of the stores were closed and dark, but a few were still open. In the distance he saw a familiar green-and-red sign all lit up: 7-Eleven. That store had ice cream. He knew that from the exact same store near his house.

He began to run, his pack bumping and jangling against his back. When he got to the 7-Eleven, he opened the door and went in.

Wandering through the aisles of candy and chips, he finally found the freezer with the ice cream inside. A cold cloud came up as he opened the case and leaned in. This time he didn't look at every one, just the ones he wanted.

"Close that case," came a voice. "You're letting all the cold out!"

Eddie snatched a bumpy-looking chocolate-covered bar and quickly slid the window closed.

He stood holding the ice cream bar, his heart beating hard.

What to do?

Pay.

At the counter he unzipped his pack and took out a fistful of coins.

"Do you know where Lucy is?" he asked the store lady as she pushed him his change.

The lady looked at him as if she didn't hear what he'd said. So he asked again.

"Lucy who?" The lady was really big around the middle and had a heart picture on her arm.

Lucy had another name, but Eddie could not remember what it was. "Just Lucy," he said.

"Don't know no Just Lucy," she said. "Try that man over there. He delivers wood. Knows everybody."

But Eddie had already broken the chocolate man's rule, even though he didn't think that bus drivers and grandmothers and store ladies counted as strangers.

He leaned his weight on his left foot, then his right foot, then his left foot again, trying to think what to do.

The man who knew everybody came up to the counter, popping the top on a green can. He wore a hat as flat as a pancake and smelled like a tree. His eyes were as blue as the pieces of sea glass Eddie had found last summer on the beach.

"Kid wants to find somebody named Lucy," the store lady said.

The man who knew everybody said, "Luz? You mean Luz? Lady in the cabin across the lake? Green trim?"

That sounded sort of right. Eddie nodded.

Then the sun came out in his head again and he took Lucy's picture from his pack and showed it to the man who knew everybody.

"Yeah, that's Luz's place all right. She's my last delivery. I can give you a lift."

He waited for Eddie to say something, so Eddie had to, even though the man who knew everybody was a stranger.

"Okay," he said, and followed the man out the door.

He didn't know if he was doing the right thing, or even a good thing. He only knew one thing for sure. That Lucy would be really proud that he'd come all this way all by himself.

And she would be so, so happy to see him.

22

"Here comes Oscar now."

Lucy looked up from Megan's April issue of *Teen People*. Grams was at the door, looking out.

Lucy got up and went to the door. A pickup truck came bumping up the drive. The truck stopped and Oscar the wood man got out.

"Brought you a visitor," he said.

He opened the passenger door and out came Eddie.

"Lucy!" cried Eddie, throwing up his stubby arms.

Eddie? How could it possibly be Eddie? Lucy blinked, trying to pull herself out of the dream.

Oscar handed Eddie his backpack. "Found him down at the 7-Eleven. Said he was looking for Lucy. I figured that was you, Luz."

"Eddie?" said Lucy. "What are you *doing* here?"

Eddie loomed over Lucy, wearing his biggest grin. "I came to see you. I came on the dog bus!" He hopped and flapped.

"By yourself? You came by yourself?"

Eddie shook his head. "Not by myself. My friend the chocolate man came on the bus, too. And Peter the twin's grandmother. And *lots* of people!"

Oscar began unloading and stacking the wood.

"Hi, Eddie," said Grams, extending her hand. "I'm Luz, Lucy's grandmother. It's so nice to meet you. Won't you come in?"

Lucy pulled on her grandmother's arm. "Grams! He's not supposed to be here!"

"Yes," said Grams. "I gathered that. But he is. Come inside, Eddie. We'll have some tea, shall we?"

Eddie took three steps into the house and stopped dead. Staring down at him was the chopped-off head of Bambi's father.

"That's Rudolph," said Lucy. "Don't be afraid. He doesn't bite."

Eddie's eyes were as wide as they could get. "Rudolph the red-nosed reindeer?"

"Um, no, not that one. Another Rudolph," Lucy said, crossing her fingers.

How was this happening? How could Eddie have taken the bus all by himself? Did his mother know where he was? Who was the chocolate man? Who was Peter the twin?

Lucy's head swam with questions as her heart began to sink. However he had managed the trip, Eddie did not belong here. This was her week with Grams, a time for private talks and special trips to the island, for walking along the lake and counting the stars. How could Eddie fit into any of that? He couldn't, that's how. They'd have to get him right back on that bus, or call his mother to come and get him.

"Come and sit down, Eddie," Grams said. "Tell us all about your trip."

"I didn't trip," said Eddie.

"She means the bus ride," grumbled Lucy.

So Eddie launched right into the story of his magic bus ride. His two magic bus rides. The chocolate man with the ear wires, the boy who called him dummy, the head with the water, the tiger claw lady, the zillions and zillions of doughnuts machine, the dog bus riding away, his money all over the floor, the doughnut girl with brown hair like Lucy's, the grandfather bus driver who let him ride without a ticket, the cars and trucks and buildings, the man who knew everybody who gave him a ride up the hill. "And then I came here!" he said, grinning.

Grams smiled the whole time. "My! What a journey!" she said. "Tell me, does your mother know you're here?"

"Sure!" he said.

"Eddie," Lucy warned.

Eddie frowned. He hung his head and rubbed his thumb where the skin was red and raw.

"Why don't we give her a call?" said Grams, as if she had just come up with the best idea ever. She got up and went to the telephone. "What's your telephone number, Eddie?"

Red-faced, Eddie pinched his lips together.

"You know your phone number, Eddie," said Lucy.

After a minute of twisting his hands together, Eddie mumbled the number.

Grams lifted the receiver.

"Her name is Mrs. Munch," said Lucy, and breathed a sigh of relief. Eddie's mother, frantic by now, would hop right in her car and break all the speed limits getting to Crescent Lake. As far as Lucy was concerned, Mrs. Munch couldn't get here fast enough. She listened to her grandmother's side of the conversation while Eddie rubbed his thumb.

"Mrs. Munch?" said Grams. "I'm Lucy Crandall's grandmother, Luz Ortega. Your son, Eddie, has found his way to my house in Crescent Lake— Yes. Yes, I'm sure it's him. Mrs. Munch? It's all right." Grams covered the mouthpiece, glancing over at Lucy. "Poor woman. She's nearly hysterical." She uncovered the mouthpiece. "Eddie's perfectly fine, not a scratch on him. The police? No. He came with Oscar, the wood delivery man. Yes. Yes. I assure you, your son is fine. You will? About six hours. Mrs. Munch? You must be exhausted with worry. Why don't you come up tomorrow when you're fresh?"

"Grams!" cried Lucy. "No!"

"Yes. Yes, of course. If your car isn't working properly, you're better off taking it to the shop and driving a loaner. Eddie is perfectly welcome to stay with us until you can get here safely. Wednesday? Of course. No, no trouble. Eddie won't be in the way. We're happy for the company."

"Sure we are," said Lucy, in a sour-lemon voice.

"Bye now," said Grams, replacing the receiver.

She came over to the couch and sat down next to Eddie. "Eddie? Your mother said you may stay two nights, while she gets your car repaired. Is that all right with you?"

Up popped Eddie's head, all the anguish wiped from his face. "Sure!"

"Grams!" cried Lucy. "*Two* nights?"

"You can sleep right here on the couch." Grams patted the cushions. "And now I'll bet you're hungry enough to eat a horse."

All the color drained from Eddie's face.

"Oh, dear. I didn't really mean that," said Grams. "It's an expression. How about a peanut butter and jelly sandwich?"

"Okay," said Eddie. "One for me and one for Lucy."

"I'm not hungry," Lucy said in her flat voice. "I'm going for a walk."

"Me, too!" cried Eddie, hopping up.

"Why don't you stay with me and have your sandwich?" said Grams, reading Lucy's mind. "Lucy needs to be alone for a little while."

"Okay," said Eddie.

Stuffing her hands deep into her pockets, Lucy went down through the trees, kicking up pine needles and clouds of dust. Angry tears rushed into her eyes and she brushed them away. How could her grandmother do this? Only five days with Grams left, and now Eddie was plopped right in the middle of it like a big fat frog.

How could Grams so easily give up her precious time with Lucy? She'd actually said those exact words—*precious time*—to Lucy's mother. Tears trickled down Lucy's face and she brushed at them angrily.

She walked quickly alongside the lake, a cold wind at her back. Waves ruffled the dark water. Lucy's sneakers were wet, her toes cold. She had planned on staying out long enough to make her grandmother worry.

Which was immature. When you were twelve, weren't you supposed to *act* like twelve?

She turned around and went back up through the trees. An owl hooted and another one answered. She would have a talk with her grandmother privately, a grownup conversation. She would tell Grams that her feelings were hurt. She was jealous, that's all. Jealous that Grams would give up her time with Lucy for another person. First Erika, now Eddie.

On second thought, Lucy decided, she would not speak to her grandmother. She wouldn't open her mouth for the rest of the day. Grams was being totally unfair. She'd arranged for Eddie to stay without asking Lucy how she felt about it, or talking it over with her, or anything.

Lucy stomped up the hill and into the house, letting the screen door bang behind her.

Eddie was sitting at the table, munching his sandwich. "Lucy!" he cried with his mouth full, as if she'd been gone for a week.

Her grandmother smiled. "How was the walk?"

Lucy went straight to the phone and dialed Megan's number, something she'd decided she wasn't going to do. Her grandmother lived on a very tight budget, and long-distance was expensive.

Megan answered. "Hello?"

"Hi. It's me."

"Lucy! Where are you? I tried to call but it's like you're on the moon! Even the operator couldn't get you."

"It's a black hole," said Lucy. Sad as that was, it felt true.

"You sound really down."

"I am. It's boring. Just like you said. Maybe I'll come home early."

"Great!" said Megan. Then she paused. "Oh," she said. "There's something else. Is it okay with you if Alandra hangs out with us? She's really nice. We thought she was a snot, but she isn't."

"I don't care," said Lucy. But she did. A lot.

"Good. If anybody knows about being popular, it's Alandra."

Lucy listened to the lines buzzing.

"Lucy?"

"Yeah?"

"What's number three? Quick!"

"Huh?"

"The twelve top tips, silly! Earth to Lucy!"

Lucy's mind tried feebly to remember number three of the twelve top tips, but then gave up. It didn't seem worth the effort.

"I've gotta go, Megan. My grandmother needs me to do something."

The sadness on her grandmother's face as Lucy turned from the telephone almost broke her heart.

23

Lucy went to the couch and flopped down, crossing her arms over her chest.

Eddie put down his sandwich. "Are you sad, Lucy?"

Lucy shook her head. "No," she said, and then she felt guilty. All summer long she'd encouraged Eddie to tell the truth about his feelings, and here she was, lying again. "A little," she said.

"Because you didn't see me for such a long time?"

Lucy almost cracked a grin. Eddie with his moon face and golden eyes, his fart jokes and his sweetness. No matter how much he exasperated her, how bored she'd gotten doing his puzzles, playing his silly games, teaching the ABC's over and over, he always managed to get a giggle out of her somehow. He was like the little brother she never got, a big, goofy, exasperating little brother.

"Well, I know you're exhausted, Eddie," said Grams, "because Lucy and I sure are. Let's make you a cozy bed on the couch. Did you bring your pj's?"

Eddie unzipped his pack and dumped it out on the

table. "Yes! Pj's!" he said, waving the striped bottoms in the air.

Lucy watched her grandmother make a place for Eddie to bed down. There would be no fire tonight. No tea and special talk. Instead of helping her grandmother, as she knew she should do, Lucy went straight to bed.

***

"Chocolate chips!"

Lucy's eyes snapped open. Then her heart sank. Eddie.

Rubbing sleep out of her eyes, she shuffled into the kitchen. There was her grandmother standing on a step stool, rummaging through a cupboard. "I think we've got some somewhere," she said. "Ah! Here they are." She turned, clutching a yellow-and-brown package.

"Careful, Grams!" cried Lucy. She held out her hand and guided her grandmother down.

"Thank you, dear," said Grams. "Eddie had the most marvelous idea. Chocolate chip pancakes. Have you ever heard of such a thing?"

"Everybody knows about chocolate chip pancakes," said Lucy.

Grams looked surprised. "They do? Well, let's see." She opened the package. "Do we just dump them straight into the batter?"

"No!" cried Eddie. "I do it! I do it!" He took the package from Grams as if it were a football and wrapped his arms around it. "You make the pancakes and I make the faces."

Grams poured three circles of batter onto the griddle. Then, very carefully, Eddie made three faces with chocolate chip eyes, noses, and mouths. "This one is you, Lucy," he said, pointing to the pancake with the biggest smile.

Was that the way he really saw her? It wasn't the way she saw herself.

Could she ever be the girl who smiled?

The pancakes were gooey and delicious. Grams made three more and then three more after that.

Lucy washed and dried the dishes. Eddie went into the bathroom and came out wearing a T-shirt with a dinosaur on it and a pair of khaki shorts. "Wanna play cars, Lucy?" he said. Then his face fell. "Oh, no!"

"What?" said Lucy.

"I didn't bring my cars!" Eddie's face was the mask of tragedy.

"It's all right," said Lucy. The last thing she wanted to do was play cars. "We can do something else."

"Why don't we work with the clay?" said Grams.

Eddie clapped his hands. "Sure thing!" he said.

Grams washed and dried her hands. Then she led the way out to the shed, her hand on Lucy's back letting her granddaughter know she understood, as she always understood, Lucy's mixed feelings.

Grams cut off a chunk of clay for each of them. Then she got right to work on her wheel. Eddie watched her with his mouth open. As her clay began to take the shape of a bowl, he blinked as if he couldn't believe his eyes.

By the time Grams cut the bowl off the wheel and set it on the shelf, Eddie's mouth was dry from hanging open.

He looked over at Lucy, whose hands were making a snake that grew longer and shrank smaller as she rolled. Then she coiled the snake around itself until it became a bumpy bowl.

"Can I do that?" he said.

Lucy heard her mother's sigh coming out of her own mouth. "I guess," she said. She showed Eddie how to make a ball with the clay and roll the ball under his hands. Biting his tongue, he got right to work.

Lucy watched Eddie for a while, thinking about the long trip he'd made all by himself just so that he could see her. It couldn't have been easy. He must have been scared all the time. Why had he done it?

He thought they were friends, that's why. And they were, weren't they? Friends cared about what happened to each other. What if Eddie had gotten lost on the way or, worse, kidnapped? What if he'd simply disappeared from the face of the earth and she never saw him again?

Lucy couldn't stand to think any more about that, so she grabbed another piece of clay and rolled the thought right out of her mind.

All of Eddie's attention was fixed on his snakes. He was trying to see how long and skinny he could make one without breaking it. He didn't want to make a snake bowl. He wanted to make animals. After a while he gathered up all of his clay and made some little round balls with it.

Lucy made another boring coil pot, then she watched her grandmother, who was working with that same deep concentration that Eddie seemed to come by naturally.

She turned to check on Eddie. She blinked. Was she really seeing what she thought she was seeing?

Tongue out, Eddie was leaning over a tiny brown clay mouse, his fat fingers delicate as butterflies lighting on a flower and lifting off again.

Lucy didn't want to break his concentration, so she touched her grandmother's arm and nodded toward Eddie.

"Oh!" said her grandmother.

Eddie lifted his moon face. "It's a mouse," he said. "His name is Peter. Peter Mouse."

Lucy and Grams stared at Peter Mouse in amazement. He was perfect, a perfect little mouse with his nose in the air, tiny round ears, and a long thin tail. Lucy half expected him to squeak.

"That's great, Eddie," she said. She wondered now why they'd never worked with clay or even Play-Doh. Eddie had all this talent inside him just waiting to get out.

Eddie shrugged. "It's just a mouse," he said, and squished it.

Lucy yelped. "No! Eddie!"

Grams put a hand on Lucy's arm to quiet her. They both stood watching him work. Another mouse in the making. No, not a mouse. A rabbit, complete with two long, perfect ears and a tiny round ball for a tail.

"It's amazing," Grams said quietly. "Where did you learn to do this, Eddie?"

But Eddie, lost in his little clay world, didn't answer.

Lucy shrugged. "I sure don't know." Did Eddie learn sculpting in his special school? She didn't think so, but where else? Did his mother teach him? "Maybe nobody taught him. Maybe he just knows how."

"That could very well be," said Grams.

"Don't squish it!" cried Lucy as Eddie with a big sigh sat back to study his rabbit.

"Okay, Lucy. I won't," he said. "Can I have a drink? This clay makes me thirsty."

They went into the house, where Grams poured three glasses of cold lemonade. "I'll whip up a batch of chocolate chip cookies," she said. "Then we'll take a walk down to the lake. Would you like that, Eddie?"

Cookies. Lake. "Yes!" cried Eddie. "Can we take a ride in the boat?"

Lucy and Grams looked at each other. "Maybe tomorrow," said Grams.

Eddie's face fell. His mother said "maybe tomorrow" a lot. Sometimes it meant "no, never" and sometimes it meant he could have it the next day if he stopped asking so much. He worried all this like a squirrel with a nut, while Lucy's grandmother whirred her mixer through the cookie dough.

Chewing his tongue, Eddie thought about asking for a boat ride again but decided to be patient. "Can I lick the bowl?" he said instead.

"Okay," said Lucy. "But I get the beaters."

"Let's wait to bake these cookies," said Grams. "It's a lovely day. Let's go down to the water." She went to the door.

122

"We'd better preheat the oven," said Lucy. "So it will be ready when we come back."

"Oh," said Grams, turning. "Didn't I already do that?"

She went to the oven and bent to turn the dial. "Where should I set it?" She looked up at Lucy, a confused expression on her face.

How many times had her grandmother made chocolate chip cookies? A hundred?

"Three seventy-five, Grams," said Lucy. "You remember."

"Of course I do!" said Grams. She whipped the dial to the right temperature. Then she led the way out the door, her head high.

"Hold hands," said Eddie, stepping between Lucy and Grams. They swung arms down to the lake.

The lake was sparkling as if it were filled with diamonds. Eddie looked up and down the shore for a sailboat. All he saw was a pointy metal thing that had rolled over on its belly like a turtle.

"See that island, Eddie?" said Lucy. "That's where Grams and I go in the canoe." Immediately she wanted to snatch her words back. Now Eddie would want to go out to the island. He could swim but not very well. Grams would never let him go all the way out there.

Eddie looked at the land poking up out of the diamond lake. "Let's go there!" he said.

"Maybe we can take a little ride," Lucy said. "Grams, would that be all right? Just in the shallow part?"

Grams frowned as she looked out at the lake. "It's a little rough this morning," she said. "If it's calm tomorrow we'll give it a try. But now it's time for lunch. What would you like, Eddie? A sandwich? Peanut butter and jelly?"

"Peanut butter and cream cheese and banana!" said Eddie.

Grams looked over at Lucy.

Lucy shrugged. "It's what he likes," said Lucy.

"Well," said Grams, "we'll see what we can rustle up."

"Cows!" cried Eddie. "We can rustle up some cows!"

Grams slid a tray of cookies into the oven. Lucy got out the Monopoly game. She set the board on the floor.

"I'm the car!" cried Eddie, diving into the box. Lucy chose the shoe. She set both pieces on Go. Then she counted out the money.

Monopoly was a long game, but not too long with Eddie. Either he cheated, sneaking extra money from the box and taking extra turns, or he tossed all the money in the air to watch it flutter down.

Lucy had explained the rules over and over. She explained what cheating was and why it was bad. She always finished with, "Nobody will want to play with you, Eddie."

"*You* will," he said. And he kept on playing his own game, sulking when Lucy snatched the dice away, singing the pufferbelly song when he landed on a railroad, and laughing himself into a coughing fit when he landed in jail.

"Lunch is ready," said Grams.

Eddie was up in a flash and sitting in "his" chair.

Grams set a plate of half sandwiches on the table.

Eddie grabbed one and took a big bite. Then he took a close look at what was left. "No banana," he said.

"It's pretend banana," said Grams, winking at Lucy.

"Oh," said Eddie. He took another bite. "No cream cheese," he said.

Lucy giggled. "It's pretend cream cheese."

"Look!" said Eddie, holding up his finger smeared with jelly. "Real jelly!" Without another word, he ate three more sandwich halves.

Grams refilled Eddie's milk and set a plate of chocolate chip cookies still gooey from the oven right in front of him.

He snatched one up and stuffed it into his mouth.

"Eddie!" said Lucy. "Take it easy."

"Mmmph," said Eddie, washing the cookie down with a swallow of milk.

Yesterday and today had been the happiest days of his whole life. First the magic bus ride, then finding Lucy and Grams, then making clay animals, and now eating melty chocolate chip cookies. He liked Grams. In fact, he loved Grams. He could live with Grams forever.

But would his mother let him? He didn't think so. She didn't have anybody to live with but the goldfish and the whirligigs. Nobody to talk to except on the telephone.

And anyway, Lucy didn't live here with Grams. She

lived in Goleta, California, just like he did. Four blocks away. She could get to his house fast as anything on her bike.

Grams took the sandwich plate and glasses to the sink. "I think it's time to unload the kiln, Lucy."

"My bear pot!" said Lucy. "I almost forgot about it."

Eddie was making car noises, racing his Monopoly car around the board.

"We'll be in the back, Eddie," said Grams.

Lucy dashed out the door. She couldn't wait to see her beautiful bear pot.

Grams touched the sides of the kiln to make sure it wasn't hot. Then she and Lucy began to remove bricks, stacking them next to the kiln.

Grams reached into the kiln. Lucy's pot was the first one to come out.

"Is that it?" said Lucy. "Is that my bear pot?"

"It is," said Grams. "Your first effort, as they say."

The gray-and-blue pot had blackish brown streaks dripping down from the rim like a rain of mud. "Where are the bears?"

Grams turned the pot in her hands. "Well," she said with a chuckle, "they're running for their lives, it looks like."

But Lucy didn't laugh. Art wasn't fun. It was hard. And she was no artist. She never would be. A big lump formed in her throat. This week was supposed to have been perfect, but it wasn't. Nothing was turning out like she'd expected.

"We'll have to get you back on the wheel," her grandmother said. "Glazing is only part of it. Like frosting a cake."

"Not in *this* life," muttered Lucy.

"What?" said Grams.

"Nothing."

They wrapped the pots in Bubble Wrap and put them in cardboard boxes. All except for Lucy's bear pot, which Grams said she wanted to keep. Lucy knew this was only because the pot would never sell. With its brown clots and streaks, it didn't look anything like the others. It was a total mess.

Lucy took it into the pottery shed and put it on the shelf. Then she stuck another pot in front of it, one of her grandmother's "mistakes," which looked perfectly fine to Lucy.

"I'll never be an artist," she said to the pots.

"Is it very important to you?" asked Grams, who had come up behind her.

Lucy turned. She thought. "Yes."

"Then you will be. And Luz?"

"Yes?"

Hands clasping Lucy's shoulders, she looked intently into her eyes. "Each of us is an artist in our own way."

"Everybody?"

"Of course." She smiled. "You knew that, didn't you?"

Lucy slowly nodded her head. And then she smiled. "I think I did."

"Eddie? Wake up."

Eddie opened his eyes. He didn't know where he was. But there was his friend Lucy, standing over him. He remembered playing Monopoly and reading books and drawing and then saying a big NO to a nap. But then everybody else took one, so he laid his head down on the couch and here he still was.

"It's time for dinner."

He sniffed the air. Something smelled like dinner all right. He got up and stretched really big.

In the middle of the table was a big bowl of salad. Eddie looked down at his meat loaf and mashed potatoes. "Cold peas," he said.

"Cold peas, please," said Lucy.

Puzzled, Grams looked over at Lucy.

"Frozen peas," Lucy explained. "That's how he eats them. Frozen."

Grams chuckled. "You're in luck, Eddie. I just happen to have a package of peas in the freezer. I had Erika bring it when I sprained my ankle." She got up, found the peas in the freezer, and shook some onto Eddie's plate.

"You sprained your ankle?" Lucy's chest got tight. "You didn't tell us you sprained your ankle!"

Grams frowned. "Just a strain. I don't tell you every little thing, you know. Your mother would never get any sleep."

In the silence they could hear Eddie's peas crunching between his teeth.

"You could tell *me*," Lucy said. "I wouldn't tell anybody."

"All I'd do is worry you, Lucy Luz." Grams smiled and laid her hand on Lucy's.

"That's okay," said Lucy. "I like to worry."

Grams frowned. "Nobody likes to worry."

Eddie pushed away from the table. "I'm fed up!" he said, patting his belly.

Lucy and Grams laughed. Eddie didn't know what was so funny, but he laughed anyway because he liked to hear himself. His laughs were like bubbles that came popping up from his tummy and out his mouth and then went sailing all over the room. He was a great laugher, a champion laugher. Lucy said so. His laughs made laughs come out of her. Sometimes they laughed until the tears came.

While Eddie washed the dishes, Lucy dried them. He was super-careful with Grams's dishes that Lucy said Grams made on her kicking wheel. Sometimes he just couldn't put a dish down because it was so beautiful. One plate had birds, a bowl had streamers, and another plate had crosses. Grams could do anything. He stood staring at a dripping plate with three wavy tree trunks on it, *his* plate, until Lucy took it away to dry.

Someday he would make a whole bunch of dishes just like Grams, only his would have animals on them. Every animal you could think of. Elephants and lions and rabbits . . .

"Let's go down by the water," said Grams. "It's a beautiful evening."

The lake was calm and still, the color of the night sky. Stars were everywhere, reflected in the water and twinkling above it light-years away. Lucy thought about standing outside the rec center with Justin and pointing out the constellations. Her heart raced when she thought about what happened after that, Justin holding two empty paper cups, his shirt soaked with Dr Pepper. She hoped he wasn't mad at her. It wasn't really her fault. It wasn't anybody's fault.

Eddie was looking up at the sky, when a star popped out and winked right at him. He was so happy that little golden sparks started bouncing off his heart.

"There's Jupiter," said Grams.

"Where?" said Lucy and Eddie together.

"There," said Grams. "You can tell it's a planet because it isn't blinking."

"I like the ones that blink better," said Eddie.

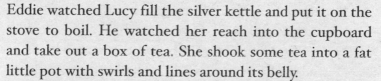

Eddie watched Lucy fill the silver kettle and put it on the stove to boil. He watched her reach into the cupboard and take out a box of tea. She shook some tea into a fat little pot with swirls and lines around its belly.

"Tea time!" he said.

Lucy set out three mugs. She poured the whistling water into the pot.

Crack!

Eddie whirled around. Grams was standing under Rudolph in front of the fireplace. She had bent herself over and was pushing a black stick into a huge fire that cracked and hissed like a dragon.

Lucy took the mugs and teapot on a tray to a little table next to the couch.

"Come on," she said, sitting down next to Grams.

But Eddie didn't like the looks of that dragon fire, not one bit. He stood behind the couch until the fire got smaller and not so noisy. Then he sat down next to Lucy on the couch.

They played What Do You See in the Fire?

Grams saw a wizard "with a long golden cloak and a staff made of jade."

Lucy saw giraffes leaping and dancing.

"Dragons," said Eddie. "Fierce monster dragons." He shuddered. "Ugly fierce monster dragons."

"Now I see ballet dancers," said Grams.

"And I see hula dancers!" said Lucy.

"Dragons," said Eddie. "Ugly fierce monster dragons."

"I like dragons," said Lucy. "They're huge and beautiful and strong—"

"And they eat little children," said Eddie.

Lucy scoffed. "Who told you that?"

"The TV told me. The TV knows everything."

"I wouldn't be so sure," said Grams, taking a sip of her tea.

"Let's watch TV!" said Eddie.

"No TV here," said Lucy.

Eddie was incredulous. No TV? How could you have a house without a TV in it? How could you watch *Sponge-Bob SquarePants* without a TV?

"I'm not going to live here forever," he said.

"Only until tomorrow," said Grams. She set down her mug and yawned. "I think I'll turn in," she said. "Big day coming up. You can make up a bed for Eddie, can't you, Lucy?"

Lucy said she could.

Grams patted Lucy's knee. Then she got up and went out to the sleeping porch.

"It's not my bedtime," said Eddie.

"Okay. Drink your tea. It's good." She sipped from her mug.

Eddie took a sip of his tea and spat it back in the cup. "It's yucky!" he said. "It tastes like dirt."

"It does not. It tastes like flowers. It's chamomile."

"I don't like to drink flowers," said Eddie, setting down his mug.

"What *do* you like? Peppermint? Green tea?"

"Games," said Eddie. "Let's play What Do You Want to Be When You Grow Up?"

"Okay. But just for a little while. You first."

"I wanna be a fireman," said Eddie. "A fireman doctor bus driver that has lots of animals."

"I want to be a fish," said Lucy.

Eddie whooped. "You can't be a fish! A girl can't be a fish!"

"What about a mermaid? Huh? How about that?"

"A girl with a fishtail? Like in *The Little Mermaid*?"

"Exactly," said Lucy.

"Okay," said Eddie. "Then I will be the captain of a giant fishing boat and I will catch you in my net."

"And I will bite the net with my shark teeth and swim away."

"No fair! You're not a shark. You're a girl fish."

"A brave strong beautiful mermaid," said Lucy. "With teeth like a shark."

Eddie crossed his arms. "I don't want to play this game anymore. I don't like sharks."

"Okay."

"But what do you want to be? Really truly. Be something nice."

Lucy thought. Then she said what was most true. "I want to be an artist. Like Grams."

Eddie clapped his hands. "Me too! I wanna be an artist fireman doctor with one million animals and four million mermaid fish." Frowning, he thought about that. "With no teeth."

Grams's fire licked at the remnants of a log that broke in half, shooting sparks into the chimney. Eddie jumped. A wind came up and rattled the door.

"It's all right," said Lucy. "It's just the wind."

Eddie sat back. "Do you love it here?"

"Yes."

"I love it, too," he said. "I love it this much." He spread his arms wide.

They sat staring at the fire for what seemed to Lucy like a long time. She yawned. Then Eddie yawned. "I'm not sleepy," he said, but when Lucy looked over, his eyes were closed and his chin had dropped to his chest.

"Eddie?"

Eddie was snoring, but not like her father, who sounded like a rusty saw. Little pig snorts. Lucy started to giggle. Then Eddie, fast asleep, began sliding toward her. She pushed her hands against the weight of him but he kept on coming, so she took her hands away and let him fall. Now he was sleeping crooked, his head on the couch and his feet on the floor.

Lucy picked up his feet and, grunting, set them on the couch.

Shoes. She should take off his shoes. Grams wouldn't want to have shoes on her couch.

But that was just too bad. Lucy wasn't about to take off Eddie's stinky shoes, not in this life!

She looked down at his sleeping face. He was such a kid, such a little kid. But there was more to Eddie than that. There was a whole world inside him that nobody really knew. People took one look at the shape of his eyes, his round face, and stubby arms and decided he was dumb. Not all of them. Not his teachers. But strangers did. She saw it in their eyes.

Eddie didn't see it. Sometimes he got very quiet, though, so maybe he did. Eddie wasn't dumb. He was kind and good and funny. He wasn't just a job—he was a friend.

Wasn't he?

She thought about Megan. And Alandra, who would be her new friend. Eddie wouldn't fit in. He wouldn't be popular. Not that popular was everything. Still, it was pretty important. Didn't Megan's sister say so?

Lucy could just imagine what would happen if Eddie tried to hang out with Lucy and Megan at school.

He would have to find some other friends. There would be plenty of kids at school happy to hang out with him.

Wouldn't there?

She laid an afghan over Eddie and tiptoed out of the room, taking her troubled thoughts to bed.

Lucy awoke to her favorite smell, pan-cakes, and to the sound of Eddie laughing. Her heart lifted. Then it dropped. Then it found a good place to hang out and stayed there.

"We're going in the boat! We're going in the boat!" sang Eddie as she came into the big room.

"The Owl and the Pussy-cat went to sea?" said Grams, encouraging Lucy to join in.

So, as she'd done so many times as a child, Lucy said the next line. "In a beautiful pea green boat."

Eddie, eyes wide, saw it all, cats, owls, and cold peas in a green boat.

Grams did the next line: "They took some honey, and plenty of money . . ."

"Money!" cried Eddie, remembering that he'd put something else, something very special, inside the pouch with his money. "Lucy! Your bracelet!"

He stumbled up and ran to the couch. He returned with his backpack, his amber eyes sparkling.

"My bracelet? You've got my bracelet?" Lucy's hand went to her mouth as if she'd already said too much. What if it wasn't true? That would be like losing the bracelet twice.

Eddie fumbled through the coins in the zippered compartment. He took out his hand and put his eyes real close. Where was it? He dumped out the pack. Out came the coins, and they rolled all over the table. A few dropped to the floor.

No bracelet.

"Eddie?"

Eddie froze.

"Where is it?" Lucy felt her throat constrict, as if she were about to choke.

"I have it!"

"Where?"

"In here! In here!"

Eddie held his pack upside down and shook it. Out came his pj's, his ten pairs of rolled-up socks, his T-shirt and underwear, and the Bic pens still in their wrapper.

"Where?"

Eddie flapped the pack in the air. "In here! In here!"

Grams came out of the bathroom. "What's going on?"

"Eddie lost my bracelet," said Lucy dismally.

"I didn't! I didn't!" Eddie hopped around. He flapped his hands. "I came all the way to bring your special bracelet. And I wasn't even afraid, only a little."

Cold sweat swept over his body. He ran for the back door. Throwing it open, he stumbled down the steps and down through the trees, falling once and getting up again. He didn't lose the bracelet. He didn't. He found the bracelet. Where was the bracelet?

Lucy watched from the door.

Grams laid her hand on Lucy's shoulder. "You'd better go after him."

"My bracelet," Lucy said.

"Does he swim?"

"My bracelet," said Lucy.

"Go on," said Grams, giving Lucy a nudge. "I don't see him now."

So Lucy started down after Eddie, who she knew would be hiding somewhere in the trees.

Did Eddie ever really have the bracelet, or was he just using it as an excuse to see her? Had he lost it somewhere on the way? On the bus? Down a toilet? Was somebody else wearing Lucy's bracelet right this minute? Admiring the tiny golden hearts? Thinking she was the world's luckiest girl? Was the bracelet down some drainpipe never to be seen again? Did a homeless person find it and trade it for food?

What would she tell Megan?

Lucy began looking behind trees. "Eddie?"

High above, a hawk answered.

"Eddie! I'm not playing. Answer me."

Beyond the trees the lake glittered its secrets.

It was dark under the turtle shell and wet. Eddie lay on his belly in the mud, his head in his arms. His brain was playing ping-pong with questions and answers instead of little white balls.

Did he have the bracelet?

He did.

Was the bracelet lost?

It was.

Did he lose the bracelet?

He didn't.

A ball bounced off the table. He began again.

Was the bracelet lost?

It was . . .

Now he would never get a ride in the boat. Lucy's grandmother would think he always lost things. If she took him for a boat ride, he would lose the boat. He had left his house and lost his own self! Now his mother would be furious. She might even spank him, if she could catch him. He would run and hide under his bed and she would get her broom and poke to make him come out.

His whole life was a terrible terrible thing.

He tried to roll over and knocked his head hard on the shell.

"Eddie?"

Lucy's brown eyes peered under the shell.

"Come out of there," she said. She grabbed the rim of the canoe and tried to lift it. "I can't do it," she said. "You have to help."

Eddie stood up with the turtle shell over him. It slid off and banged to the ground.

"How did you get under the boat?"

"It's not a boat," said Eddie. "It's a turtle shell."

"Whatever," said Lucy, sounding exactly like Megan. "Come on. You're all wet."

"It's not a boat," insisted Eddie. "It's a turtle shell."

"It's a boat, Eddie. It's called a canoe."

Eddie stared at the canoe in amazement. "I never saw a boat like that."

"Come on," said Lucy. She started trudging back up the hill, turning once to make sure he was behind her.

"Oh, dear," said Grams as they came into the house. "I think somebody needs a shower. Let's get some clean clothes for you, Eddie, and I'll show you how to work the shower."

Lucy threw herself down onto the sofa, crossing her arms. In her journal, if she ever got one started, she would call this week the Flippity Flop Roller Coaster Week. Things kept going up and down, good times, bad times, followed by good things, followed by bad things. If the rest of her life was like this, she would be permanently exhausted. She would have to take a hundred vitamins and naps every day just to keep up with it.

Her grandmother came over and sat beside her. "Poor boy. I think he really had your bracelet, don't you?"

Lucy nodded her bent head.

"He came all this way just to give it to you, and then—?"

"He lost it."

"Yes."

They could hear Eddie banging his elbows on the walls of the shower he was too big for. "I'm a little teapot, short and stout," he sang off-key.

Grams laughed. "He's a sweet boy."

Lucy frowned. "I know."

"We promised him a boat ride."

"I know."

Grams stood and gave Lucy a hand up. "I'll wrap some cookies to take along." She started toward the cupboard.

"Eddie ate them all."

Grams turned around, surprised. "He did? When?"

"I don't know, but they're gone."

"Well!" said Grams. Her glasses sitting crooked on her nose made her look a little crazy. "He's a growing boy, isn't he."

"He's not supposed to be growing *out*!"

"No, I suppose not."

Eddie came out of the bathroom wearing the pants he showed up in and a clean T-shirt with a picture of a polar bear cub. SAVE MY PLANET, said the caption over its head. Eddie's hair poked up like porcupine quills. "All clean!" he said, and stuck his hands down into his pockets. His eyes opened wider than Lucy had ever seen them. Out came his right hand. In it was her bracelet.

Lucy squealed.

"Oh!" said Grams.

Eddie just stared at the bracelet as if he'd performed the greatest magic trick in the world without knowing how. "It's your friendship bracelet!" he said. Then he gave it to Lucy, who stared at the bracelet as if it had dropped out of the sky.

Something solid settled into place as Lucy slid the

bracelet onto her wrist. "Thank you, Eddie," she said, blinking back tears. "Thanks for bringing it all this way."

"All this way," said Eddie. A thrill of fear danced down his backbone. How had he done it? How had he come a zillion miles without his mother? Without getting lost? He thought for what seemed like a very long time.

"Maybe the bracelet brought *me*," he said at last.

Lucy and Grams pulled their paddles slowly through the water, skirting the shore. On the floor between them sat Eddie, wearing Grandpa's life vest, as round and proud as a happy king.

"Ducks!" he cried, as a family of six paddled past.

Lucy pointed at the female. "That's you, Grams," she said. "Cool, calm, and collected."

Grams shook her head. "You just can't see what's going on below the surface," she said. "That lady is paddling like crazy just to keep her head above water."

"I'm *not* a little teapot," said Eddie.

Grams and Lucy looked at Eddie, who had the most determined look on his face.

"You certainly are not a little teapot," said Grams.

"I'm a duck," he said, spreading his wings. "And I own this whole pond."

Eddie waved to the man and boy who were fishing from Oscar's dock. "We're going for a boat ride!" he cried.

The man waved, but the boy had a puzzled expression

on his face. Wasn't it obvious the fat kid was going for a boat ride?

"We're going for a boat ride!" cried Lucy. "We're paddling to Alaska!"

"We're an owl and a pussycat!" yelled Eddie. Then he looked at Grams and thought hard. The poem had only two animals in it.

"And Lady McDuck," said Grams.

"And Lady McDonald!" cried Eddie.

They went slowly along the shore, north, then south, and then north again until Grams's arms gave out. She and Lucy pulled the paddles in and let the canoe drift. They sang the five songs that Eddie knew by heart and taught him "You Are My Sunshine," all three verses. Lucy sang in almost perfect harmony.

Eddie threw a fit when it came time to go in, but it wasn't a very big fit and nobody got their underwear in a twist, not even Eddie, who had forgotten to put his on.

"This is what I call a good day!" he said when they were trudging up the hill.

Grams stopped in her tracks. Eyebrows raised, she looked at Lucy. "That's what your grandfather always said."

Lucy did the *Twilight Zone* theme.

"Stop!" said Grams. "That tune gives me the willies."

"I think that's your mother now, Eddie," said Grams, peering through the screen. She opened the door and stepped outside.

Eddie jumped up and bolted for the bathroom. He slammed the door behind him.

Lucy heard the lock click. "Eddie?"

"Tell her to go away," he said.

"Hi, Mrs. Munch," said Lucy to an empty room. "Eddie says you have to go away."

The doorknob turned. Out popped Eddie's head. "Is she gone?"

"Your mother's been really worried about you, Eddie. It wasn't a very good thing you did, running away. I mean, it was a good thing because of my bracelet, but a bad thing because—" If she told him what was true—that he could have been kidnapped and lost forever—would he ever try anything on his own again? "Because . . . because—"

"I know, Lucy," he said. "I'm *not* a baby."

"Eddie!" Mrs. Munch flew through the door, her arms wide.

Eddie stood pinned inside his mother's arms. "Hi, Mom! Guess what I did!"

His mother dropped her arms and scowled. "I know what you did," she said. "You ran away from home. You were a very naughty boy."

"No, I didn't! I didn't run. I walked and I looked both ways twice and I rode on the bus. I didn't run once!" And then he remembered. "Except when the witch chased me out of the dirt."

"Promise me you will never do that again," said his mother.

"Promise, cross my heart," said Eddie happily. For all he knew, he might never see that witch again.

Lucy helped Eddie stuff his backpack while Grams showed Mrs. Munch her pottery shed and kiln. When they came back in, Eddie's mother had a stripe of clay down her slacks. On Grams's palm, like it was sniffing the air for food, sat Eddie's rabbit. "Shall I fire it for you, Eddie?" said Grams. "Or would you like to take it with you?"

"Don't throw the rabbit in the fire!" Eddie cried.

"Oh, dear, no. I didn't mean—"

Lucy laid her hand on Eddie's arm. "If it goes through the fire, it gets strong," she explained. "And then it won't break."

"Oh, well, okay then," said Eddie. "But be really really careful."

"As if it were my own," said Grams.

Eddie shrugged. "You can have it."

Grams looked stricken. "Oh, no! I didn't mean I wanted to keep it."

"It's okay. You can," said Eddie.

"He's a very generous boy," said his mother. "He'll give you the shirt off his back."

"Oh, no I won't!" said Eddie. "My tummy will get cold."

Eddie followed his mother out to the car and got in. Framed in the open window was his happy moon face, his crooked-tooth hundred-watt smile. "Hey, Lucy! See you later—"

"Alligator!" said Lucy.

Eddie waved as the car pulled away. "In a while—"

Lucy waved back. "Crocodile!"

She and Grams watched the car until it was out of sight.

"Well!" said Grams. "Life sure has a funny way of throwing you curveballs, doesn't it?"

"But we're good catchers. Aren't we, Grams?"

"The best. Give me a high five!"

"That's a low five, Grams. You have to hold your hand up. Like this."

They slapped hands.

"And now it's time for my nap," said Grams.

✳

After a light supper of canned peaches and cottage cheese, Lucy and Grams went outside to stargaze. Grams had turned off the house lights, switching on the flashlight only long enough to settle on the back steps. Darkness snuggled in around them like a fleece coat.

An owl hooted from somewhere in the trees. The lake buzzed and clicked and whirred as if all the bugs and frogs were tuning up for a symphony.

Lucy jumped when Wild Thing came up and rubbed against her leg.

"There you are!" said Grams. She reached for Wild Thing, but he disappeared in a flash of gray.

"What do you think the stars are all talking about?" said Grams after a while.

Lucy thought about it. "I don't know. Something important, I guess. Something really big."

They named the constellations they knew. Then they made up names for the ones Grams wasn't sure about. Mister Blink, Cruella Minor, Snoop Catty Cat, Starry Potter.

"I like to think there's a star up there for everyone who's passed on," said Grams.

"Which one's Grandpa?"

"Right there," said Grams, pointing. "That very bright one. The one who keeps talking after everybody else has shut up." She laughed. "Do you remember what a great talker your grandfather was?"

"I just remember that he called me Lulu. I didn't like that. But I was afraid to tell him. He was really big."

"And gentle and funny. I hope you remember that, too."

Lucy remembered that his eyes twinkled and that he had a big white mustache. For years she thought he might be Santa Claus, and that nobody was telling her.

"I didn't think I could stand it when he died," said Grams. "I wanted to die, too. Just curl up in a ball and never wake up." Grams pulled her skirt down around her ankles to warm her legs. "Your grandfather always seemed to know what to do, to have the answer for everything. I didn't think I was strong enough to live without him."

"But you were," said Lucy. She didn't like to think of her grandmother as weak and afraid. It frightened her.

"Oh, yes, I was strong. But it took a while to trust that I had my own answers."

It had always seemed to Lucy that other people knew much more than she did. Even people her own age, like

Megan and Justin. "How *did* you know when you had the answers, Grams?"

"Well, I didn't always. I made a lot of mistakes. And then, when I finally had it mostly figured out—?" She laughed. "I was old."

Lucy snuggled closer to her grandmother. Someday her grandmother would have a star, too. But Lucy didn't want to think about that either, about the time when she wouldn't have her grandmother anymore.

27

Lucy awoke to a scratching sound and sat up. Wild Thing was stretching himself against the screen. She slid out of bed and let the cat in.

Her grandmother's bed was empty, the covers thrown back.

She went into the house, the big room gray and shadowy in the moonlight. The bathroom door stood partly open.

"Grams?"

She went to the back door, which she had made sure to lock. It was open. Only the screen door stood between her and whatever might be out there in the night.

"Grams?"

She opened the door. Something skittered into the bushes. Skunks? She called again, her voice hollowing out into the dark shapes of trees. She found Grams's big yellow flashlight and scanned the yard, the trees like a line of soldiers bordering the land.

Then she stepped outside.

"Grams?" Louder this time.

Below was the lake, a silver path laid across it by the moon. As she watched, a small white figure floated onto the path.

Lucy took off running down through the trees, the yellow light like a tennis ball bouncing ahead.

Grams in her long white nightgown. It *had* to be. "Grams!"

But the figure had disappeared.

Had she walked out into the water? Would she drown before Lucy could reach her?

Tripping over a branch, Lucy went down on all fours, the flashlight bouncing out of her hands.

She got up and brushed herself off.

The figure in white was gone.

Lucy breathed hard. The air filling her chest felt sharp with cold. Had she imagined it all? She knew she couldn't be dreaming because her scratched hands stung.

The white figure floated out from behind a tree. Grams, it *was* Grams, her long gray hair loose and drifting about her shoulders.

Lucy moved slowly now, knowing instinctively that if her grandmother was sleepwalking it would not be good to frighten her.

Grams seemed to be caught up in an argument, stabbing her finger at someone who was only in her mind.

"It's not that way at all, not at all! No, that is not what I said!"

She stood ankle-deep in the water, the hem of her nightgown soaked.

Lucy took a step closer. "Grams?"

Her grandmother stopped. The anger left her eyes. Now she looked merely puzzled.

She looked at Lucy as if she'd never seen her before.

"Grams? It's me, Lucy. Luz."

Grams stuck her hands on her hipbones. "Well? Are they coming?"

"Who? Nobody's coming. It's just me, Grams."

Lucy held out her hand, and saw that it was shaking.

Her grandmother stared at Lucy's hand. "I don't think they're running the trains this late, do you?"

Grams looked like Grams, only she didn't. Lucy had never been so frightened in her life, and yet it was just Grams, the person she loved most in the whole world.

"Grams," said Lucy quietly. "It's me, Lucy. We need to go home now."

Her grandmother frowned. "What are you doing out here in your pajamas? Come here, child, you'll catch your death. It's so cold."

She stepped from the lake and held out her arms. Lucy went into them, swallowing hard to keep from crying.

"I told you never to leave the house by yourself. Didn't I, Susie?"

"Grams, it's me. Lucy." The tears came in a rush. She couldn't stop them.

Her grandmother held her at arm's length and studied her face.

"We need to go home now, Grams." Lucy helped her grandmother into her slippers. She put her arm around her grandmother's thin back and led her, step by slow step, up the hill to the house.

"Home, home on the range," sang her grandmother in her warbly voice. It was funny, but it wasn't.

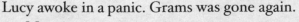

Lucy watched her grandmother climb into bed, turn on her side, and fall immediately asleep. She herself sat up, the pillow against her back. She didn't know the time. Close to morning, she guessed. Not pitch-dark but not light either.

She would stay awake all night. She would make sure her grandmother didn't get up and go wandering off again, and tomorrow, first thing, she would call her mother. She would do it while Grams was out in her shed. Her parents would come racing right up.

And then what? They'd take Lucy home, of course. But what good would that do? Grams would be all alone again. Well, alone except for Erika, who wasn't much help.

Maybe she wouldn't call after all. Calling would only make things worse.

Lucy's mind bounced from calling to not calling until it wore her out. Her eyes began to close, and then her chin dropped.

She pinched herself on the arm and sat up straighter.

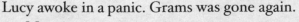

Lucy awoke in a panic. Grams was gone again.
Morning.

The smell of pancakes.

Lucy closed her eyes and felt like crying. Instead, she got up and went into the kitchen.

"Good morning, darling," said Grams, as if it were any old morning. "I've used the last egg in these cakes. They'll be delicious. Better put eggs on the list."

She scooped two cakes off the griddle and handed them on a plate to Lucy.

Did Grams know? Did she remember? Should Lucy tell her? Tell someone?

Her parents. She should call her parents. That was the right thing to do. First the fire, now her grandmother wandering off by herself in the middle of the night.

She should call. But she wouldn't. It was her job to take care of Grams, as it had been Grams's job once to care for her. Calling would mean she had failed.

She took her plate to the table and sat down.

"Lucy?" said Grams, sitting across the table. "I mean Luz. I'm not very good at this name change, I warned you." She poured syrup onto her pancake. "I had the strangest dream last night, so real I could almost touch it. Do you know the kind?"

Lucy nodded. She was sure the pancakes would be great, but she suddenly had no appetite for them.

"Your grandfather was being so inconsiderate . . . Well, he could be, you know. He kept insisting that the train from Paris . . ." She laid down her fork. Lucy watched her face go pale. "It wasn't a dream, was it?"

Lucy shook her head. She looked down at her plate

because she could not bear to look into her grand-mother's eyes.

"Oh, Luz," Grams said, sitting back. "I must have scared you silly."

Lucy shrugged. "You were sleepwalking, that's all. My friend Megan—"

"No, honey, I wasn't. I wish it were that simple." She sighed. "I'm afraid I—"

But Lucy wouldn't let her finish. "We'll get a big bolt for the door," she said. Trying to stay awake last night, she had worked out a solution. "That way I'd hear the bolt slide if you got up."

Her grandmother smiled a troubled smile. "Good idea," she said. "I knew you'd think of something."

But it wasn't the answer. Lucy knew it, but told herself she didn't. "I'm a light sleeper," she said. "Any old thing wakes me right up."

"Well, I'm glad that's settled," said Grams. She stood, the hem of her nightgown filthy from lake mud. "I'd better get some clothes on. We need to make an early start."

"For the island?" said Lucy. "Are you sure we should go?"

"Of course!" said Grams. "Why wouldn't we?"

Lucy put on her best pair of jeans and a new bright blue T-shirt, but when she looked into the mirror her eyes looked dull and red. Like Erika's. Or like a girl who had hardly slept, a worried twelve-year-old girl who just might be in over her head.

It was a cool, almost cold morning with a stiff breeze. Hiding behind a gray cloudy sky, the sun seemed in no hurry to make an appearance. Lucy's Windbreaker under her life vest kept her mostly warm as she dug her paddle into the water. Her grandmother wore a scarf under her straw hat and her old green cardigan. Did she even own another one? A warm one? For Christmas they would have to buy her a Windbreaker with a fleece lining, green like that sweater, which was nearly the color of her eyes.

On their first trip out, Lucy had concentrated so hard on getting the paddling right that she hadn't asked Grams all the questions she wanted to ask: Who owned the three small cabins strung out along the lake? She knew one of them belonged to Oscar, but what about the other two? How deep was the lake? What happened to the fish in the winter?

But now she had no breath for questions. All her energy went into dipping the paddle and pushing the canoe into the wind. Cold water splashed up from her paddle and stiffened her fingers. Her nose and lips felt numb.

"Hard going," her grandmother muttered once with her head down, but that was all.

Closer to the island, the wind was blocked and the going got easier. They beached the canoe and pulled it as far above the waterline as they could, its metal bottom screaming over the rough stones.

A small brown rabbit poked its head out of the weeds, then turned and disappeared.

Hands on her hips, Grams looked up at the sky. "I wasn't paying attention to the weather this morning," she said. "I really am slipping, you know. Suppose it rains?"

"I guess we'll get wet," said Lucy cheerfully. "We'll have to crawl in with the foxes."

"We'll have to find them first." Grams was smiling the way she did the instant Lucy jumped out of the car. Lucy had her grandmother back, and all to herself.

They went up the same trail, Grams leading, her knapsack hanging from her shoulders. In it were PB&J's, sketchbooks, some charcoal, colored pencils, and a Snickers bar. Lucy carried the water.

Halfway to the top, they stopped to rest.

"Look!" said Grams, pointing up. "A pair of redtails looking for lunch."

The hawks made lazy circles in the air, as if it didn't much matter what was below. But of course it did.

By the time they reached the flat rock at the top, Lucy was warm enough to take off her jacket. She sat on the rock and looked down to where the foxes might be. "Would the hawks go after baby foxes?"

"If the kits were small enough, they would. These should be several months old, too big to be prey. And of course their parents will be on guard."

Grams sat and opened her sketchbook. She began to draw an outline of the rocks. The hawks were gone from the sky but still in Lucy's mind. She opened her sketchbook and tried to draw them, but it was hard. Her hawks looked flat and lifeless.

Then she decided to draw them from above, as if she were the sun or maybe God looking down. Below widespread wings she drew the grass and a tiny mouse running for its life. She liked this one.

Then she looked over at her grandmother's sketch, which was full of shading and detail. "Oh, Grams," she said. "That's so good." She closed her sketchbook.

Her grandmother made a curved line with the edge of her charcoal. "Well, I've been doing this forever," she said. "I should have learned something by now. Let's see what you've done."

Lucy opened to her sketch, which didn't look finished now.

"I like that perspective, Luz," said Grams. "I wouldn't have thought of that."

Lucy was surprised. "You wouldn't?"

Grams went back to shading the rocks.

Lucy gave her mouse a shadow.

What had become of the "go-away" mouse Eddie had

given her? At the bottom of the hamper in her bedroom maybe, or lost. What if he had asked her about it? What would she have said?

On Hat Island everything seemed so far away: the pool, the new yard, Justin, her parents, Waldo, even Eddie and Megan. It was like she and Grams were in a world all their own.

"I never thought about being an artist until this week," she said, smudging the shadow with her finger the way her grandmother did. "But maybe I'll be one when I grow up. Did you go to art school, Grams?"

"I didn't," said Grams. Regret edged her voice. "Well, I took a class here and there. I think art school would have been wonderful."

"I guess it would. But what if people didn't like what you did?"

Strands of silver hair danced around her grandmother's head. "What people?"

"Oh, you know. The teachers and the other students. What if they thought your stuff was junk?"

"Oh, you couldn't let that stop you," said Grams firmly. She closed her sketchbook and slid it into the knapsack. "You don't do art for other people. It isn't a popularity contest."

"It's important to be popular," said Lucy, hearing Megan in her voice. She didn't expect her grandmother to agree.

"Yes, I suppose it is. It certainly feels important, doesn't it?"

"I wouldn't want to be like Erika."

"No, of course you wouldn't. But you aren't like Erika. I should think you'd have scads of friends."

"Well, I don't," said Lucy.

"Oh? Why is that?"

"I'm not sure." And then, suddenly she was. "I'm a little shy," she said. "I can't just go up to people and talk to them."

"No?" Grams had taken off her ancient hiking boots and her socks. Her feet were long and very white with crooked yellow toenails.

"What if, you know, they didn't want to be my friend?"

"I guess you'd try somebody else." She smiled at Lucy. "Somebody with better taste."

Her grandmother opened the water bottle and passed it over.

Lucy took a sip and passed it back. "I'd like to be popular for a little while," she said. "Just to know how it feels."

"You could just decide that you are." Grams brushed an ant off her arm. "Act like all the popular kids. Do what they do." She peered intently at Lucy. "What is it they do, anyway?"

Lucy shrugged. "I'm not sure. They smile a lot, and they're always around other popular kids. And they talk on their cell phones, like, *all* the time."

"I guess you could try that."

"You're always full of good ideas, Grams."

"They were your ideas, Luz. The thing is, if you look inside your heart, you'll always know the right thing to do."

"I guess so," said Lucy. But looking inside her heart didn't seem to have a whole lot to do with being popular.

29

A wind came up and they moved into the shelter of a large rock. There were words chiseled into the flat side of it: MANDO + JAMIE, RED SOX RULE, and ROCK OUT, which made them laugh. They watched for foxes, but saw only rabbits and lizards.

Lucy considered scratching DODGERS RULE on the rock, but she didn't have anything to scratch with.

"Tell me another secret, Grams," said Lucy.

"Oh, no you don't. You owe me one."

Lucy thought. She had two secrets in mind, and both were hard to tell. But the first was worse because it was about being a bad person. So she told the other one.

"I kissed a boy," she said.

She half expected her grandmother to be shocked, as her mother would have been. But she wasn't.

"You did? Was it good?"

"Not very." The kiss had happened in April at Megan's birthday party during a game of spin the bottle. Charlie Taggart, a boy nicer than he was cute, had spun and to Lucy's horror the bottle had pointed to her. While everybody cheered, she and Charlie touched lips. Then Megan's mother came downstairs and broke up the game.

It wasn't much of a kiss, but she supposed she had to count it.

"First kisses are seldom good," said Grams. "But we remember them all our lives for some reason."

"Your turn," said Lucy.

Grams thought for a while, a mischievous smile at the corners of her lips. "I went topless on a beach in France."

"Grams! No!" Lucy giggled. "Were there people around?"

"Oh, yes. Lots of them. All the women were barebreasted. It was sort of funny, really. All those different kinds of breasts. Big ones, little ones, floppy ones."

"I can't believe you did that!"

"Well, it was sort of awful at first. All I could think about was who was looking at me. But nobody was. And then I sort of got my feelings hurt. Wasn't I pretty enough? Weren't my breasts big enough?"

"Oh, Grams," said Lucy. She could hardly believe her ears. Her grandmother bare-breasted in public!

"And then I stopped thinking about it. The sun was warm and I began to relax. A lovely experience, really. Very freeing."

A drop of rain fell on Lucy's head, then another on her arm. Her grandmother held out her hand. "Uh-oh," she said. "We'd better scoot."

Lucy stood. She looked up at the sky. Tiny raindrops prickled her face. Her grandmother hurriedly pulled on her socks and boots. She got to her feet and shouldered the knapsack.

On the shore below, the canoe looked very small and far away.

"We'll have to hurry," said Grams, but she had to pick her way carefully and slowly down the narrow trail. The dark sky suddenly lit up.

"Lightning," said Grams. "I was afraid of that."

Lucy counted. "One one thousand, two one thousand . . ." A rumble of thunder. "It's close," she said.

And then the rain hit, all at once, as if a bucket in the sky had been turned upside down. Cold rain pelted their backs as they rounded the last bend in the trail.

"We need to get to the canoe," yelled her grandmother over the roar of the wind. She had bent herself over as if to make a smaller target for the rain. Her sweater and blouse were drenched. Her wet slacks clung to her thin legs.

A crack of lightning opened the sky. Lucy slipped and nearly fell. "Careful, Grams!" she yelled.

"We need to find shelter," said her grandmother, stopping and turning to look back at Lucy. The sides of her straw hat were flattened against her head and she was shivering.

"Up there!" she said, pointing to something in the weeds. But Lucy was too short to see it. "We'll have to get up to that cave."

Grams reached for Lucy's hand, then had to let it go as they began to climb again. The trail was muddy, the rocks slippery. They had to grab handfuls of weeds and spindly bushes to pull themselves along. The cold rain sheeted down Lucy's face. She was shivering now, deep inside herself.

If her grandmother slid, Lucy would have to catch her or they would both tumble backward down the trail.

A flash of lightning lit up the hillside like an old black-and-white movie. Thunder rumbled as if rocks were rolling downhill.

Grams stopped and looked around, turning in a circle. "Where is it?" she cried. She stumbled off the trail and began heading away from where she'd said the cave was.

"Grams! This way!"

Her grandmother turned back, a wild, frightened look on her face. "Where? Where are we going?"

Lucy held out her hand and led her grandmother back onto the muddy trail. "Follow me," she said.

She didn't know where the cave was, exactly, only that it wasn't in the direction her grandmother had been going.

She pushed through the wet grasses, held the bushes back, and coaxed her grandmother along. But there was no shelter, no place to hide from the pelting rain. Her grandmother began to whimper. Lucy turned and put both arms around her.

Lightning was everywhere now, forking in jagged intersecting lines across the dark sky. They were easy targets for it.

They had to find shelter.

"Come on, Grams!" cried Lucy when her grandmother stopped to gaze up at the sky as if she didn't know why all this was happening and was very annoyed with it. Her hat had slipped off and hung by its cord down her back. The wet scarf clung to her head.

"They aren't coming, are they?" said Grams. "Grady. And the other one."

But Lucy didn't know who Grady was, and it frightened her even more than the lightning. Her chest felt tight. Tears gathered to release. She pulled her grandmother along, not knowing if there was even a cave ahead.

And then there it was, appearing out of the weeds like an open mouth. Lucy bent to look inside. Empty, empty and dark, but dry.

She crawled in and put out a hand for her grandmother.

From inside, the cave was a small upside-down bowl. Lucy was glad it wasn't deep, and that it was unoccupied.

"Ohdearohdearohdear," her grandmother muttered.

"Sit down, Grams," said Lucy. "It's okay. We're okay now."

Flashes of lightning were followed immediately by a rumble of thunder. The storm was right above them.

Her grandmother sat and began plucking at her wet slacks. "What has it all come to?" she said, shaking her head back and forth. She was shaking all over and her lips were blue.

They needed a fire but had no way to start one. There was paper in the sketchbooks, but none of it was dry, and they had no matches.

Lucy took the almost-empty water bottle out of the pack, opened it, and held it to her grandmother's lips.

Her grandmother began to laugh. "Water," she said, in her normal, no-nonsense voice. "We aren't going to run out of that. Are we, Lucy girl?" She squeezed Lucy's arm and took a small sip of the water. "This is what you call a real sorry state of affairs, Lucy," she said. "*Luz*. I did it again, didn't I?"

"It's all right, Grams. It doesn't matter."

What mattered was that her grandmother had returned from wherever she had gone, the scary lost place where she didn't remember things.

Grams nodded, as if she'd decided something. "This will blow over," she said. "These summer storms never last."

Another crack and an immediate boom echoed across the sky.

"We got off the trail for a bit, that's all. But I knew the cave was here." Then after a minute: "Did I do it again?"

"Get lost?"

"In my head. Yes."

"Just for a little while. Not long. Don't worry."

But Lucy could see that her grandmother couldn't let it go.

Huddled together, they watched the rain falling in sheets at the mouth of the cave, silvery against a black sky. For a long time, they didn't speak. Then her grandmother said, "This is a problem."

For a moment, Lucy didn't know which grandmother

was speaking, the lost one or the normal one. She felt her shoulders tensing.

"I have become a problem."

"What do you mean, Grams?" Lucy's voice sounded careful, the way it did with Eddie when she wasn't sure what he was talking about or what he might do.

Her grandmother rested her cheek on the top of Lucy's head. "My mind is going, Luz."

Lucy almost said, "Going where?" She wanted to make a joke of it. She didn't want to hear that her grandmother was sick, or that her mind was.

"I haven't wanted to face it. I thought we could have this one last summer in the cabin and—"

Lucy jumped like she did whenever the fire-drill buzzer went off at school. "What do you mean, 'last'?"

"Oh, Lucy," said Grams, not bothering this time to correct herself. If she remembered. "I wasn't going to tell you yet. I didn't want to spoil our time together. I'm putting the cabin up for sale."

"No! Why?"

"I'm going to move." She glanced quickly at Lucy's face and looked away. "Into this perfectly lovely place. I had intended to show you the brochure. You know, when I told you. When the time was right. But then Eddie came and—"

Lucy, hugging her knees, laid her forehead down. "No," she said. "No."

Her grandmother's arm came around her. "We'll still be able to see each other," she said. "And we'll talk on the telephone, just like always. I know you'll miss the old place. So will I."

"No," said Lucy, like a much younger child. She rolled her forehead back and forth across her sharp kneecaps. "What about the canoe? What about this island? And the foxes? We haven't even seen the foxes!"

She began to cry. The canoe didn't matter. Even the foxes didn't matter. The loss would be greater than that. It loomed over her now like the clouds before the storm, dark and threatening.

"I'm sorry, darling," said Grams. "I am so sorry."

Lucy wanted to say the right thing, which was the true thing, which was to say that none of it was her grandmother's fault. But she couldn't. She shrugged out from under her grandmother's arm. She moved away, hugging herself. She wasn't angry with her grandmother. The thing she was angry with was much bigger than that. It was, maybe, God.

After a while, they ate their PB&J's, still dry in their baggies, and shared the Snickers bar, staring out at the rain.

"What is it like, Grams, when your mind goes?" Lucy wasn't sure then that she should have asked, but she needed to know. How could she help if she didn't understand?

Her grandmother laid her sandwich down. "It's very confusing at first," she said. "A little like a dream, I suppose, but not a good one. I think I'm somewhere else, someplace I once lived. Or I don't know where I am at all.

169

Or who I am. And then I panic, which makes it all worse. In the old days, they called this sort of thing 'spells,' which doesn't sound so bad."

She frowned. She tried to read Lucy's face. "You don't need to hear all this."

"I do, Grams. I need to know. Or it's kind of scary for me, too."

"Yes. Yes, of course it is."

"Can't you take something? Some medicine?"

"Yes, there's medication. I'm taking it now. I thought it was helping. I hadn't had a spell for several weeks. I thought it would be all right for you to come, and so I convinced your parents." She sighed. "I haven't been entirely honest with them. And see where that's gotten us!" She held a hand out to the rain.

"It isn't just the spells. I'm not as aware of things as I used to be. The weather, for one. Before, I'd have known a storm was on its way."

She rolled the knapsack into a wet pillow and laid her head down on it. Lucy spooned against her, and they tried to keep each other warm.

Lucy thought about the canoe filling up with water. She worried about how to get help. When Erika came with the groceries, would she guess where they had gone? She was their only hope, but a thin one.

"Do you think Erika will tell somebody we're out here?"

"She'd have to notice the canoe was gone," said Grams. "But even then, no one's likely to cross the lake in this storm. We're stuck, I'm afraid, until it passes on."

The ground was hard. Lucy brushed away a stone digging into her side. She listened to her grandmother's soft, steady breathing and knew she had fallen asleep. The thunder rumbled off into the distance, and there was only the occasional flash of lightning. But the rain came down as if it meant to flood the world.

Lucy awoke and sat up. The world was quiet. She'd had a strange dream but couldn't remember it. The world was *very* quiet. For a minute she didn't know where she was. The cave, the storm, her grandmother asleep on the ground. Then she recognized the feeling her grandmother had tried to explain. She had felt the panic rising like floodwater, but now it too was gone.

The rain had stopped. She crawled to the mouth of the cave and looked out. Across the rippled lake stood the line of pine trees and the three cabins, smoke rising from one of them. It wasn't yet morning. Or if it was, the sun had hidden itself behind an overcast sky. She let her grandmother sleep.

She crawled out and stretched. Turning, she looked across the lake, which seemed in this direction to have no end. She was stiff and sore. Hungry. And then, as she watched, a hint of brightness along the horizon. First a brief dazzle of light, and then above a line of dark gray clouds a brilliant band of orange as the sun began to rise.

She went back into the cave and nudged her grand-mother's shoulder. "Wake up, Grams."

Her grandmother stirred and opened her eyes. "Hmmmm," she said.

"Look! It's the sun!" said Lucy, who had never seen anything in her life more beautiful.

They sat arm in arm as the sky filled with bands of orange and purple, charcoal gray, and a deeper purple her grandmother said was heliotrope.

"I wish we could see the sunrise together every morning forever!" said Lucy.

Grams gave Lucy's shoulder a squeeze before letting go. "That would be wonderful," she said.

Grams combed her fingers through her long gray hair and remade her ponytail. "We'd better get to the canoe while the weather holds."

After helping her grandmother out of the cave, Lucy reached inside for the knapsack, pulling the thin straps over her shoulders. They went in search of the trail they'd come up, but every beginning led to a dead end.

"As soon as we see the canoe, we'll know right where we are," said Grams.

They pushed through the weeds, making several more false starts. Her grandmother sat down on a rock, breathing hard.

"I think we're lost, Grams." Wherever Lucy turned looked the same. Same weeds, same rocks. The island was bigger than it looked.

After a rest they set off again, but Grams kept dropping farther and farther behind. Lucy had to stop and wait.

The lake was an empty blue, the sun harsh. Her grandmother had taken off her cardigan and slung it around her shoulders. Her straw hat sat crooked on her head.

Whenever they came to a place where they could get a glimpse of the shore, they looked down, expecting to see their canoe. But the canoe was gone. Swept away by the storm, Lucy guessed, but she didn't want to say it.

She began to think they would never get back.

How long could they last without water, without food? This seemed a thing that people, even people her age, should know. But she didn't. If she asked Grams, she'd only worry her.

Once, she thought she heard Grams talking to herself, but it was only the wind.

"We'll have to make our way down without a trail," Grams said. She looked exhausted.

They went down through the weeds, which slapped at their faces and soaked their clothes all over again. The ground was chunked up and muddy, full of gopher holes. They held hands when they could.

Once, a hawk screeched overhead and Lucy jumped. They watched it dive, and when it rose again into the air, something small and limp was hanging from its beak.

"Gopher," Grams said.

Lucy cheered. "Good! Only eight thousand more to go."

They picked their way carefully down the hillside.

Lucy, deep in thought, didn't hear the plane until it was almost overhead. Grams hadn't heard it at all. Lucy took off her Windbreaker to wave at it, jumping up and down and yelling. But the small blue-and-white plane flew on.

"Maybe they'll send somebody," said Grams.

Lucy frowned. "They won't. They're supposed to tip their wings to say they saw us."

She thought about her parents then, not for the first time. She and Grams were being like her father and mother: her grandmother looked at the bright side of things, like a nice flat rock they could rest on, while Lucy pointed out all the gopher holes.

It took forever to make their way down to the narrow, stone-covered beach.

As far as they could see in both directions, no canoe.

31

They searched in vain along the water's edge.

"The canoe could be anywhere," Grams said. "Who
knows where we left it."

But there, straight across the water, tiny gray smudges
from this distance, were the three cabins. This is where
they had beached the canoe. Didn't Grams remember?

"I can't walk another step," said Grams. "We'll just
have to wait."

Without a rock to rest on, they sat on the stony
beach. But Lucy kept thinking about the canoe. What if
it hadn't floated away? What if it only got blown to another part of the island? "I'm going to keep looking,
Grams. You rest." She got up, brushed the dirt from her
seat, and took off walking.

"Don't try to go all the way around, Luz," Grams
called. "It's too far!"

Lucy's stomach felt hollow. She needed water, but the
lake water wasn't safe to drink. Some bug that started

with a G, Grams said. But she knew they would have to drink eventually, or die of thirst.

The sun blazed down on her face. She felt dizzy and shook her head to clear it. And then she began running. The canoe! Tipped on its side, tossed like a toy onto the rocks, was her grandmother's old canoe.

Lucy ran up to it. No leaks, as far as she could tell. Their life vests were gone and so were the paddles, but they had the canoe.

She ran back to Grams, already yelling before she got to her. "The canoe! I found it!"

"Oh, thank the Lord!" said Grams. She got to her feet and followed Lucy back down the beach.

"The paddles are gone, but we can find something!"

Her grandmother stopped, a stricken look on her face. "No paddles?"

"It's okay," said Lucy. She refused to think about it.

"We can't cross without paddles, Luz."

What was the matter with her normally optimistic grandmother? They had the canoe. They'd find something to paddle with. At least they'd get off the island.

With some effort they righted the canoe.

"What was that?" said Lucy. She'd heard something. A rifle shot, or maybe thunder.

Her grandmother looked out over the lake. There were clouds on the horizon.

"We can't cross anyway," her grandmother said, climbing inside the canoe, looking up at the sky. "I think we're in for another storm."

"I'm going to find those paddles," said Lucy, in what

her father called her my-way-or-the-highway voice. She stomped off, leaving her grandmother sitting in the canoe.

"Luz! Come back. Those paddles are long gone!"

But Lucy strode ahead, her hands stuffed into the pockets of her jacket. A cold wind blew straight into her face. The sun had all but disappeared.

She walked for what seemed like miles. Then she began worrying about her grandmother. What if she got lost again? What was Lucy doing, looking for some dumb paddles that were probably on their way to Alaska when her grandmother—

She spotted a weathered board just above the waterline. She ran over and picked it up, knocking off the sow bugs and one bright orange spider. Tucking the board under her arm, she hurried back along the shore. When she saw the canoe, she began to run. Where was Grams?

"Grams!"

Her grandmother lay on the floor of the canoe, curled up on her side, snoring. Lucy decided to let her rest. She would go in search of another board to paddle with, or maybe even one of the paddles.

Her grandmother opened her eyes and sat up.

"Look what I found!" Lucy held up the board.

"Wonderful!" said Grams, climbing out of the canoe. She looked up, shading her eyes. "I think the storm is moving off. Shall we make a run for it?"

By the time they dragged the canoe down the beach, her grandmother could hardly climb into it. Lucy settled herself in the stern, pushing the board into the muck and giving the canoe the nudge it needed to float. Then she took off her jacket and handed it to her grandmother. "Put it on," she said. "I won't need it."

When her grandmother didn't protest, Lucy knew how tired she was.

With the jacket wrapped around her, Grams settled herself on the floor of the canoe and laid her head on the seat.

With both hands and a lot of effort, Lucy pulled the splintered board through the water. The canoe turned in a half circle, and then all the way around when she did the same thing again.

At last she got the hang of it, paddling first on one side and then the other. But it was slow going. The wind had died, and after a while she was forced to stop. Her muscles ached, her hands stung.

Grams had fallen asleep again.

The land was a million miles away or wasn't there at all, a mirage only. She would never get them home.

After a while, she began paddling again, keeping the three cabins in her sights. But it wasn't long before she had to stop again to rest.

Grams was singing in her sleep. Lucy couldn't tell what song, only that it sounded sweet and made tears come into her eyes.

She needed to rest. She would lie beside her grandmother for just a little while. And then she would start paddling again.

Lucy awoke kicking and trying to scream.

"Shhh! You're all right." Bright blue eyes. Oscar. She was being lifted into a boat, a white motorboat with a cabin and cushioned benches.

Everything came back like a punch. The island, the storm, her grandmother wandering lost through the weeds.

Oscar had set Lucy on a blue seat cushion and now she sat straight up. "Where's Grams?"

"She's fine, fine. Not to worry. Erika's got her wrapped in a blanket. She's below."

Oscar took off his jacket and put it around Lucy's shoulders. Then he went up to start the engine. The bow lifted as the boat pushed through the water, the canoe tied on and bouncing behind.

32

They sat by a blazing fire with their usual mugs of chamomile tea, which Lucy decided tasted like damp straw. Not like dirt, as Eddie had said, and not like flowers either. But the cup was warm inside her hands and she thought she might someday even like chamomile tea, that she would drink it and remember sitting on the old broken-down sofa next to her grandmother, even though she would be sad.

How could she not be? The house would be sold, the sofa gone to the Land of Lost Sofas, and her grandmother would be at her "lovely place," which could never in a million years be as special as this cabin.

"Tell me another secret, Grams. It was your turn, remember?"

"Oh, no you don't! I distinctly remember that it was your turn. Distinctly."

"Okay, you're right," Lucy admitted. "But tell me one anyway. *Then* it'll be my turn."

Her grandmother was quiet for a little while, thinking. "I would like to have a boyfriend," she said. She looked down at Lucy with the most mischievous smile. "Does that shock you?"

"A little," Lucy admitted.

"I'd just like somebody to lift the heavy stuff, and tuck me in at night."

Lucy giggled. "Is that all?"

"Of course that's all! What did you think?" Grams's eyebrows lifted as if she were shocked.

"How about Oscar?"

"Oscar? Heavens no. He's too old."

Lucy giggled. Oscar was at least twenty years younger than Grams, at *least*.

"On second thought, he was our knight in shining armor, wasn't he?"

"Erika, too," said Lucy.

When they hadn't returned by morning, Erika had gone out looking along the lake and a good way into the woods. Then she called her father, who noticed the canoe was gone. When they were safely home, Erika heated up a can of chicken noodle soup and fussed over them like a mother hen.

"Your secret must be a humdinger if you've kept it all this time," said Grams, pushing her poker into the flames. "I'm listening."

Lucy made a face. "It isn't good."

"Tell," said Grams.

"I think I'm—" Lucy chewed her cheek. "I think I'm a bad person."

"Oh?"

"Really bad."

Her grandmother laid a hand on Lucy's knee. "What makes you think so, Luz?"

"Well, for one thing I'm rotten to Mom. I say the meanest things to her, the meanest things I can think of. Sometimes I don't even like her."

"That must feel just awful."

Lucy sat up, her hand on her chest. "I know! She probably hates me."

"I meant for *you*. It's awful when you feel that way inside."

Lucy slouched back against the pillows. "It is. It makes me feel like a bad person."

"I'm sure it does," said Grams.

"And Eddie! I can't stand to be around him. Not when it's just the two of us, but when there's other people. Not you, Grams, but other people. It's horrible! It's so embarrassing the way he looks and acts. And it's not even his fault."

"Poor Eddie," said Grams, shaking her head.

"I'm the only bad person in this whole family!" cried Lucy.

"Oh, no you're not," said Grams.

"Don't tell me you're a bad person, Grams, because you're not."

"Sure I am. We all are sometimes. Mostly good, but sometimes not. Just like everybody else. Just like you. That's what it means to be human," said Grams. "At least we have a choice."

"Sometimes it feels good to be bad," said Lucy.

"I know," said Grams.

"But then it doesn't," said Lucy.

"I know," said Grams.

They were quiet for a while, then Grams said, "It doesn't feel good that I've been less than honest with your parents. We need to tell them what happened out there, you know."

Lucy had already decided not to tell anybody but Megan. "Do we have to?"

"No, *we* don't. But *I* do. They need to know what's happening to me, Luz. And I haven't yet told them about selling the cabin."

"Grams?"

"Yes, darling?"

Lucy bit her lip, then she asked the scariest question, the one that had been on her mind for days. "What if you forget me?"

Lucy had been prepared for her grandmother to laugh, to say that forgetting Lucy could never happen in a million years. But her grandmother's face only got sad, sad and serious. "It might seem as if I've forgotten you, Lucy Luz, but in here"—she laid her hand over her heart—"I never will." She folded Lucy's hand and kissed her knuckles. "Never."

33

Grams was at her wheel before break-
fast. When Lucy went out to find her, a little worried that
she wasn't inside, her grandmother had her arm up to the
elbow inside a tall cylinder.

Lucy watched quietly until Grams sat back and let the
wheel spin slowly to a stop. She turned to smile at Lucy, a
smear of clay across her cheek, another in her gray hair,
and one more on the left lens of her glasses.

She stepped down, drew her wire under the pot, and
lifted it onto the worktable. "I woke up wanting to do
something really big," she said. "Breakfast?"

Lucy looked at the wheel. "May I try it again?"

"Of course!" said Grams, clearly delighted. "I've been
saving some special clay for you." She turned her back
and rummaged through her stash. "A magic piece."

But when she thunked it on the wheel in front of
Lucy, it looked like all the rest, a dull, reddish brown
chunk of mud.

Her grandmother gave the wheel a kick. Lucy wet her

hands and cupped the clay. Grams's hands came over hers. Together they pushed and molded the clay, Grams's cheek against Lucy's ear.

And then something happened. Lucy didn't know at first what it was. The lump of clay felt the same, and then it didn't. It went completely and absolutely still. And so did Lucy. "Grams!" she said.

But Grams said nothing. She lifted her hands and stood behind Lucy, letting her have her first centering all to herself. And then, together, they pulled up the pot.

"I had a feeling I could do it today," said Lucy. "I don't know why, but I was right." Her brow furrowed. "It's weird, sort of, the centering thing."

Her grandmother's green eyes were brighter than usual behind her clay-spattered glasses.

"It's like the whole world stops," said Lucy. "Only it doesn't. It keeps spinning, just like the wheel. It's like . . . Oh, I don't know. It's hard to explain."

"Yes."

"It was right inside me, inside my whole self."

"I know exactly what you mean," said Grams. "If I could center just one pot every day, I think I would remember who I am. I would never get lost."

"Will you take your wheel with you?"

"I don't know, Luz. I don't know if it's allowed. I'll certainly try."

"You should. I think it's important."

Grams looked into Lucy's eyes. "You're right," she said. "It *is* important. Shall I make a scene if they won't let me bring it?"

186

"*I* would!"

Grams laughed. "Then it's settled. Take me, take my wheel!"

"Let's go down to the lake one more time," said Lucy.

Hand in hand they went down through the trees. The sun was shining in a clear blue sky, the lake a deeper blue that they both tried to name: cobalt, azure, lapis, cornflower, inky, bluey, midnight.

"This would have been the perfect day for a trip to the island," Grams said with a sigh.

"But it wouldn't have been the same, Grams."

"No, it wouldn't have." Grams chuckled. "We'd have been dry and warm."

"You know what I mean."

"Yes, I know what you mean."

When they saw the boy and his father fishing in the same old spot, Lucy almost let go of her grandmother's hand. She was too old to be holding hands with anybody. Well, anybody but a boy. Instead, she gave her grandmother's hand a squeeze and got one in return.

"I'm going to miss you, Grams," she said, a catch in her throat.

"And I you, Lucy. Oh, there I go again! Luz."

They stood at the edge of the water lapping gently against the shore. In the sunlight Hat Island looked close enough to touch. Lucy searched for the cave they'd spent the night in, but couldn't find it. It seemed now like a dream.

Lucy wondered if, when school began again, she'd be asked to write about her summer. But that was a baby assignment. Still, she began to think about how she would write about going to Hat Island.

She wondered if she might someday be a writer as well as an artist, if there would be enough time in her life to do all that.

They went back to the house, made another batch of cookies, and then ate too many while they were still warm and melty. Lucy felt warm and melty inside. Happy. Grams hadn't forgotten one thing since yesterday, and maybe she wouldn't for a long time.

But that was probably what her mother called "wishful thinking."

Lucy looked around the room she loved so much. She wondered what her grandmother would take with her when she left, and what would happen to Rudolph. And who would feed Wild Thing.

She curled into a corner of the couch and listened to a cricket singing in the hearth, her grandmother filling the kettle for tea, and, before she was ready, the sound of her father's car.

Her parents came in high spirits. They each grabbed Lucy up and squeezed her as tightly as if she'd been gone for a month. They ate some cookies, and then some more cookies. Lucy took her mother outside to show her the pot she'd made almost by herself. When she tried to explain centering, her grandmother standing by, she could tell that her mother didn't get it. But Grams did, and that was enough.

The dreaded time to say goodbye came all too soon. Her father, anxious to get back for the Dodgers game, led the way to the car. When they were home, Lucy would watch the game with him. They would eat popcorn, her father would yell at the ump, and Waldo would curl up on Lucy's feet as if he'd only dreamed that she was gone.

At the car door, Grams's arms came around Lucy from behind, catching her off guard. She could feel her grandmother's warm breath on the top of her head. "And Luz?" she said, as if they'd just been talking and were still alone. "Centering? It's that place you go to when you want to know what to do, the best and right thing. It will always be there inside you when you need it."

Lucy turned and hugged her grandmother, tears wetting her grandmother's white blouse, her old green cardigan. "Oh, Grams," she said, sobbing. "I don't think I can stand it."

"You can, my darling," said Grams, rocking Lucy against her chest. "You can."

34

Lucy sat next to Megan on the low wall that ran along the quad. On the other side of Megan was Alandra, and on the other side of Alandra were two of Alandra's friends, Stephanie and Emily, who were both on their cell phones.

"Where are you?" yelled Emily. "Where? We're in the quad, dummy! You're supposed to be over here. Well, then, come!" She punched the END button on her Black-Berry, then hit another button and started talking again.

Stephanie pointed to her red phone and mouthed, "My mom," and rolled her eyes.

Megan grinned at Lucy. Lucy could read Megan's mind. Her mind was saying: *Can you believe this? Can you believe we're sitting with these girls? Can you believe we're in the popular group?* Lucy guessed all this from the way Megan was sitting, as if she were at attention. Even her pink hair, which now had turquoise tips, stuck straight up. She wanted to tell Megan to stop smiling so much. It gave her away. It made her look needy.

The quad teemed with kids, kids on phones, kids pushing one another and laughing. Seagulls dived for food scraps. A girl screamed. A boy and girl kissed in the dark passageway where the lockers were and nobody stopped them.

Lucy had taken her schedule out of her backpack a dozen times. She wanted to take it out again. She had art next and would have to find it by looking again at the map on the back of her schedule. Just this morning, between English and social studies, she had found the art room. She had put her face right up against one of the wide windows and peered in. In the corner was a kick wheel, just one, and shelves of clay and bisque-fired pots.

Emily jumped up and waved. "There they are! Candace has those jeans!" She turned to look at Stephanie, her eyes wide. "You know the ones! We saw them, remember? At Blue Bee. They're two hundred bucks!"

Lucy and Megan turned to each other. For the first time, Megan looked doubtful. Maybe they weren't in the right place after all.

Two hundred dollars? For jeans?

Megan and Lucy got introduced to Candace and Tessa as "Megan, the girl who lives down the street, and Luz, her friend." And then they were all talking at once, all except Lucy, who didn't know what to say and wanted to take her schedule out of her backpack, even though she'd look dumb doing it.

"Lucy! Lucy!"

Lucy whipped around.

"Oh, no!" cried Megan. All the girls went quiet as Eddie came stumbling up, his hands bouncing and a huge goofy grin on his face.

"Lucy! Guess what? Guess what?" He was grinning with all his gum showing and his crooked little teeth.

Lucy froze.

She was terrified for a minute that Eddie would throw his arms around her, though he had never done that. Since coming home from the cabin two days before, she'd managed to avoid him completely. Afraid his mother would ask her to hang out with Eddie again, and maybe even to be his friend at school, she didn't go near the Munches' house.

Now, seeing Eddie, she wanted to turn and run.

But she didn't.

Something happened. Something she never could have imagined. In the swirl of color and noise and laughter that spun around her, she was still, absolutely still.

Centered.

She felt herself smiling, her cheeks cool without a trace of blush.

"Hi, Eddie!" she said. "How are your classes?"

Eddie did his hopping dance while he told her all about his classes, the teachers whose names he didn't know but who gave him treats, and all his friends, and his cubby.

He went on and on about the cubby that was all his own to put his stuff in and had his picture on it so that he could find it by himself.

Emily, Stephanie, Candace, and Tessa had made a whispering huddle.

Megan stood just outside the huddle, between the girls and Lucy, who was listening to Eddie go on and on about his cubby.

The bell rang. Eddie looked around, alarmed.

A teacher came up behind him. "There you are," she said. "I've been looking for you. You're supposed to wait for Mrs. Alexander. Remember?"

"Bye, Lucy!" Eddie backed away, waving.

"Bye, Eddie. I'll see you later," said Lucy.

The girls, all but Megan and Lucy, headed off in separate directions, calling orders for where to meet and when.

"God!" cried Megan with her hands on her cheeks. She looked like the painting Grams had once shown Lucy of a weird-looking person screaming on a bridge. "That was terrible! He ruined everything!"

"Eddie?" said Lucy.

"Special Eddie!" groaned Megan. "What are you going to do?"

Lucy shrugged. "I don't know. Be his friend?" She was grinning. She couldn't help herself. It all seemed so silly. What was the big deal, anyway?

"You won't be popular now," said Megan dismally. "Did you see the way they were looking at you?"

But Lucy was anxious to find her art class. She took out her schedule and studied the map.

"Did you hear what I said?"

"I heard you."

"Doesn't it matter to you?"

Lucy looked at Megan, whose face was blotchy red.

"Oh, I give up!" cried Megan. "Wait!" she yelled, and took off at a run after Alandra.

It wasn't until after her art class, where she'd asked and gotten permission to use the wheel while all the other kids rolled coils, that Lucy began to feel sad and anxious, and then sorry. All summer before the one precious week she'd had with Grams and the Catalina trip with her parents, Lucy and Megan had been together. They'd planned their outfits, their hair, what they'd say if so-and-so did or said this or that. They'd explored the empty campus of what would become their new school, staked out the girls' bathrooms.

With straight faces they had walked ever so casually past the house of a cute eighth-grade boy whose parents were friends with Megan's parents, and then laughed so hard they almost peed their pants. They'd practiced kissing. They'd vowed eternal friendship, no matter what, no matter who else became their friend, even someday in the far future when they would each marry. Or not.

After school Lucy waited for Megan at the traffic light where they'd already planned to meet. Everything about that first day, they'd planned right down to the minute.

Everything except Eddie.

Twisting her bracelet around and around her wrist, Lucy waited until the last few kids straggled out.

No Megan.

She walked toward home by herself, biting her lip to keep the tears at bay. What a baby she was turning out to be!

"Lucy! Wait!"

Lucy stopped and turned. With a huge grin on her face, she waited for Megan to catch up.

"You'll never guess who I talked to! Chuck!"

"Who?"

"Chuck! You know."

And then Lucy remembered. Megan's parents' friends' son. The eighth-grader. "Oh!"

"We talked for like an hour! I'm sorry I'm late."

They walked toward home, Megan telling Lucy everything she and Chuck had talked about, which didn't sound all that great to Lucy—it was mostly about the summer and what they'd each done on vacation with their parents—but Megan was breathless and thrilled.

"Megs?"

"Yeah?"

Lucy bit down on her lower lip. "Does it matter that much if I'm not popular? Because I might not be. I'll probably be an art geek, like my grandmother."

"Oh, Lucy," said Megan. "Don't worry. You won't be. You'll be popular."

So Lucy let it go. It was enough to be walking home from her first day of middle school with her boy-crazy best friend. She hadn't centered a pot in her art class as she had been sure she would. She was too aware of all the other kids, bent over their clay coils. But she would try again tomorrow.

On Sunday night she called her grandmother. The phone rang and rang. Lucy's heart sank a little deeper with each ring. Then Grams answered. "I knew it was you!" she said. "I was in the shed and couldn't get here fast enough. How are you, Luz? How is seventh grade?"

So Lucy told her all about her classes, the pot she'd finally centered, about Justin, who chose a desk right next to hers in Spanish class, and at last about Eddie. That was the best part, the part she knew would make her grandmother smile.

In the four school days since that first one when Eddie had come running across the quad, Lucy had seen him everywhere, talking with everybody. It was hard to tell from some faces what the kids were thinking, but most of them seemed to like him.

It could be, it just could be, that Eddie was popular!

She and Megan still hung out with Alandra and her friends between classes, but the popular girls couldn't be found at lunch, at least not in the caf where Lucy and Megan ate.

But then Lucy wasn't looking very hard.

"Erika's staying nights now," said Grams. "She's turned into a real helper."

"That's good," said Lucy. She wanted Grams to be more specific, and maybe she would ask more next time. She would ask if Erika was watching the stove. If she was helping her grandmother come back from the scary place she went when she forgot who she was.

"She'll be a help with the packing when the cabin sells," said Grams.

"Have you gone out to look for the foxes?"

"I'll wait for you," Grams said.

But Lucy knew it would never happen now. The cabin would sell. Condos would be built in its place. Her grandmother would go to the "lovely place" and Lucy would visit her there, along with her parents, who would have to drive her. They would drink tea and Lucy would try to keep her grandmother from forgetting who she was, and who Lucy was. She would buy her grandmother a cell phone, a pink one. She would put a picture of herself on it and call her every day. She would help keep her centered.

They finally stopped talking, or Lucy did, when Grams tried to suppress a yawn and Lucy caught her at it. "I love you, my Lucy Luz," said Grams.

"I love you, too, Grams. More than anybody in the whole wide world."

She hung up, and when she turned there was her mother, caught listening. Lucy's heart clenched, but her mother smiled. "There's nobody quite like Grams, is there?" she said. She held out her arms because Lucy was weeping. And then her mother was, too.

They went into the kitchen hand in hand to have a cup of tea, plain old black tea, the kind her mother drank, with heaps of sugar and nonfat milk.

Lucy sat across from her mother at the table. "I'm going to paint one of my bedroom walls," she announced, her heart already lifting as she thought about how, beneath a sky filled with brilliant stars, she would paint two small figures sitting side by side, forever looking up at it.

Acknowledgments

The Last Best Days of Summer started as a germ of an idea in my mind and grew to become the book you are holding in your hands. What feels like magic to me now was in reality the result of a lot of hard work, a collaboration of minds and hearts that happens every day in the children's division of Farrar, Straus and Giroux and never ceases to amaze me. My deepest appreciation to Frances Foster and Lisa Graff for their brilliance, patience, and generosity. Lucy would not be here were it not for you. Thank you to Robbin Gourley and Jaclyn Sinquett, who matched artistic design to the words I wrote and made them shine. And to the copy editors, who continue to straighten my path, correct my farther/furthers, and put all my commas where they really belong—thank you. As always, my deep gratitude for the endless patience of my first editor and love, Jack Hobbs, and to my fellow fairy godsisters, Lee, Mary, Robin, and Thalia.

QUESTIONS FOR THE AUTHOR

VALERIE HOBBS

What did you want to be when you grew up?
More than anything, I wanted to be a professional ice-skater.

When did you realize you wanted to be a writer?
There wasn't any one moment of realization. It just came over me sneakily, and then I realized that I was one.

What's your first childhood memory?
Sticking my finger into an open light socket. It was almost my last memory!

What's your most embarrassing childhood memory?
Running naked out of the bathroom when the lights went off into the living room full of people. Of course, the lights came right back on and there I was.

What's your favorite childhood memory?
Christmas morning, deep snow, a "real" baby carriage and doll, a miniature piano.

As a young person, who did you look up to most?
Lad from *Lad, A Dog*, by Albert Payson Terhune. I'm serious.

What was your worst subject in school?
Math.

What was your best subject in school?
English.

What was your first job?
Selling ladies' underwear at Woolworth's.

How did you celebrate publishing your first book?
I took myself to lunch at an expensive restaurant downtown and had a glass of wine. Then I wrote notes for my next book all over the paper table cover. But I didn't write the book.

Where do you write your books?
In my "office" upstairs, which is also the TV room.

Where do you find inspiration for your writing?
Walking in Elings Park which has an ocean view and hang gliders.

Which of your characters is most like you?
They all are in some way, but Bronwyn Lewis is the most me.

What is your favorite summertime memory?
Going to stay on a farm in Upstate New York, digging up potatoes, picking raspberries (and beetles off the raspberry bushes). Making blackberry ice cream.

What do you hope readers will take away from this book?
Some understanding of those who are struggling with disability.

Where did your grandparents live?
Metuchen, New Jersey.

Where do you see Lucy in the future?
She's a teacher and plein air painter.

When you finish a book, who reads it first?
My husband, Jack.

Are you a morning person or a night owl?
Definitely morning.

What's your idea of the best meal ever?
Fresh-caught salmon from the Pacific Northwest, a glass of Jaffurs Syrah, and chocolate mousse for dessert.

Which do you like better: cats or dogs?
Dogs (but please don't tell Molly, my cat).

What do you value most in your friends?
Their ability to listen and to love me unconditionally.

Where do you go for peace and quiet?
My backyard.

What makes you laugh out loud?
My grandkids, Diego and Rafael. Just about everything they do cracks me up.

What's your favorite song?
"I Will Survive."

Who is your favorite fictional character?
Dorothea Brooke, *Middlemarch*.

What are you most afraid of?
Poverty.

What time of the year do you like best?
Fall (with spring a close second).

What is your favorite TV show?
The Office.

If you were stranded on a desert island, who would you want for company?
My husband, Jack.

If you could travel in time, where would you go?
Paris, 1920.

What's the best advice you have ever received about writing?
Write from the heart.

What do you want readers to remember about your books?
We are amazing and powerful human beings, each and every one of us. Sometimes we lose our way, but we can always find it again.

What would you do if you ever stopped writing?
Read. Travel. Whine a lot.

What do you like best about yourself?
My sense of humor.

What is your worst habit?
I fall into pessimism and believe that I will never write another book, or a good enough book.

What do you consider to be your greatest accomplishment?
Learning little by little to see the bright side of things.

Where in the world do you feel most at home?
Santa Barbara, California, and Volcano, Hawaii.

VALERIE HOBBS has written many acclaimed books for young readers, including *Sheep*, which was nominated for six state awards, and *Defiance*, which was nominated for ten. Her novel *Anything but Ordinary* was named a New York Public Library Book for the Teen Age and declared a "drama of the highest order" by *The Bulletin of the Center for Children's Books*. She lives in Santa Barbara, California, where she is a lecturer emerita at the University of California.

valeriehobbs.com